ERIC'S STORY

BRAVIG IMBS

Eric's Story

originally published as The Professor's Wife

eglantyne books

Published by Eglantyne Books ltd,

The Club Room, Conway Hall, 25 Red Lion Square, London WC1R 4RL.

www.eglantynebooks.com

All rights reserved

©2021 Eglantyne Books

ISBN 978-1-913378-07-3

Printed in the UK by Imprint Academic Ltd;

Seychelles Farm, Upton Pyne, Exeter, Devon EX5 5HY, ImprintDigital.com

A CIP record for this title is available from the British Library.

Cover and book layout and design by Eric Wright

Production team: Robert and Olivia Temple, Michael Lee, and Eric Wright

PUBLISHER'S NOTE

When this book was published in 1928, the recognition that the true location of the story was the campus of Dartmouth College at Hanover, New Hampshire, was almost immediate. All of Bravig Imbs's friends and acquaintances knew that between 1922 and 1924 he was an undergraduate at Dartmouth. (He did not finish his degree course, but left early.) Dartmouth is a highly prestigious university, the northernmost of the seven 'Ivy League' universities in America. Bravig Imbs himself was an American who was the son of Norwegian immigrants, hence his Norwegian name. As Imbs admits, the celebrities in this book are given their real names, and it is only the central Dartmouth personalities whose names are disguised. The book is essentially a record of Imbs's own experiences, and the conversations of the celebrities are believed to be accurate. In fact, it was later claimed that he wrote them down in his notebooks immediately after hearing them. Imbs calls himself Eric in the novel. One of the characters in the novel is a tiny French bulldog named Scarot. In 1977 an unsigned letter to the editor was published in the Dartmouth Alumni Magazine by someone who claimed to be the last living person who had been at one of the dinner parties described by Imbs. The person revealed that the real name of the dog was Chicot and that it was 'a horrible little dog'. The mathematics professor Rosenkranz and his wife Nadia Schulz Rosenkranz appear in the book under their real names, even though they were local to Dartmouth. The President of Dartmouth at the time of these events was Ernest Martin Hopkins, who was the 11th President between 1916 and 1945. He was highly regarded and deeply respected. But he cannot have been amused at this book, because it was officially banned from the Dartmouth Library and the Dartmouth campus, and even from the university town of Hanover. It seems that it was also banned for a time in the entire state of New Hampshire, the authorities of which did not wish their state's famous educational institution to suffer any indignity. The true identities of the Ramsons and others were recorded in lists kept in a rare book room at Dartmouth, and at one time they were kept under lock and key, though whether this remains the case is unknown. However, it has now been possible to discover the true identities of the Ramson family by extensive research, and to learn that Delia's real name was Myrtle. 'Professor Ramson' was really Professor David Campbell Kelley Lambuth (1879-1947). His wife whom he married in 1902 was Myrtle Ayres Spindle (1877-1953). Their daughter 'Jane' was really Jean Spindle Lambuth (1904-1963), hence at the time of the story she was aged 18 to 20. She later married another Professor of English at Dartmouth, Kenneth Allan Robinson (died 1968), who appears in the novel as Clarence Rollinson. David Lambuth's father was a Methodist missionary, Walter Russell Lambuth, well known in both Japan and Brazil. In 1889 he founded a university in Japan named Kwansei Gakuin (known as "Kangaku") in the city of

Nishinomiya in Hyogo Prefecture, which is still a prominent university in that country. David Lambuth himself was born in Shanghai. Both he and his son-in-law Kenneth Robinson were very well known academics with a high reputation for scholarship. Myrtle was born in Virginia, daughter of Henry Hunter Spindle and Emily Elizabeth Long Spindle. Their home was at Rockingham in Virginia.

The real "Professor Ramson", David Kelley Lambuth, about the time of his marriage to Myrtle ("Delia").

Lambuth, head of the English Deparment, in 1922, the very year that Bravig Imbs came to live in his house.

To Elliot Paul
and the cider
of Mayenne

AUTHOR'S NOTE

The scene of this story is any American college town, and the characters, aside from celebrities who are called by their actual names, are all fictional creations.

I

The Ramsons' place was called Otterby. The name was Mrs. Ramson's idea; she got it out of her favourite author, James Barrie; I remember what a shock it was when she told me she thought Barrie was a greater writer than Shakespeare. "He has the light touch," she said, "that Shakespeare never had." You remember in the first part of "'A Kiss For Cinderella', how the servant girl is accused of being a German spy - the play is in wartime - and when the policeman questions her - he had been warned beforehand that her chief characteristic was to remind you of where you came from - well, the policeman is talking to her and she told him how his buckle sparkled, he must have spat on it to make it shine so and he answered, yes, it was a way they had in Otterby. Otterby was the place where the policeman had come from, so there you are, and Mrs. Ramson said, "Call the house Otterby, for to any travelled person there will be some part of the world it will remind him of," and Myron thought it was a good idea. It really was amazing how easily he could be influenced by his wife. I saw a book he had given her on their honeymoon and it was inscribed to the "Bold Adventurer." Of course, that was a compliment and referred to a romantic incident - romantic to Delia anyway - on their honeymoon while they were in Scotland. They must have been a right pair on their honeymoon; when they were in Paris they wouldn't even take coffee at a café because people were drinking alcoholic liquors all around them. That was on account of Bishop Ramson, I suppose. Anyway, he's dead now and Mrs. Ramson rushes out to the kitchen whenever she gets emotional to have a glass of her homemade wine. But I was talking about this honeymoon trip when they were in Scotland. It seems they were walking through some deserted Scottish glen and night fell before they realized it. They weren't precisely lost, but it was a long way back and Delia was tired. She was a frail thing when she was married, from one of the best families of Virginia, and considered quite an intellectual there because she was strong for Kipling. She was so tired, though, that she wouldn't walk much farther, she said; they would have to stop for shelter at the next house. Myron was horrified because if there ever was a perfect gentleman it was he, and the idea of stopping at a strange house and asking for shelter bordered on impoliteness and was certainly a bold thing to do. But Delia, tired as she was, was insistent that she should stop, and so when they came to the house, quite a large stone one with shutters, Myron was fuming a little, but ineffectively, and Delia was the one who had to ask for shelter. It seems the people were rather shocked at first, but seeing that they were strangers and bien élevés, they invited them in, and in an hour they were lifelong friends and Mrs Ramson was so proud over this exploit that she always kept up a correspondence with these Scottish people, and their daughter Jane later visited them on her honeymoon. Only I guess Jane was a little wild in their eyes, for she did flaunt her vain Paris gowns and prompted the old lady to write Delia about the younger generation and their mad ways, and secretly Delia was pleased because, for all Myron was modern and taught Conrad in his classroom, she was at heart a conventionalist and loved the idea that she was a high lady of a landed estate.

Otterby, of course, was no great property, and there were no trees on it when they bought the lot, and the house looked so very naked with the scraggly little poplars that lined the drive, but that was partly Myron's idea because he wanted to get as close to a flesh color as possible for the house. He would almost bite his teeth when he pronounced the words, "luscious, sensuous flesh tones," and his full beard with pointed mustachios was as precise as his pronunciation. Of course, being a professor, and an English professor at that, accounted for the fantastically perfect way he talked, and in class he would make the worst poem in the world sound like a masterpiece. "I must confess," he would say (it was his most favourite expression) after finishing a poem, perhaps a Browning monologue -he did those especially well, though the Pre-Raphaelites were his real delight - "I must confess," he would say, "that this poem gets me." He liked to use the word "handle" too. Some of his critical phrases got current in the town because they could be used in so many ways. Especially the one about Sinclair Lewis. Professor Ramson was always talking about virility and he took great pride in being punctual and precise. "Main Street?" he said when someone asked him about that book. "Ah, Sinclair Lewis - good camera, good lens, but -" You could use it a hundred ways. When you fell down skiing someone was sure to say, "Good camera, good lens, but-" and the prize chaperones at the fraternity dances were always "Good camera, good lens, but -"

The carpenters all liked him when Otterby was being built, because for all his way of talking they could see he was a good scout just the same and it was only because he was swell and a professor. He really got very friendly with one of the carpenters--he was the head one, Barton, and he was a bird. I liked him from the beginning. I was sitting in the bathroom scraping the paper off the new porcelain tub, as the water hadn't been installed yet, and this fellow in overalls and free and easy ways with him dropped in and said to me, "Hello, bud, I hear you're from Chicago, my favourite city." I was surprised because he talked with an Eastern accent, but he explained he had been born in Vermont, so that was all right. He sat down on the bathtub so as to hinder me from working, and we had a long talk about Chicago. He told me where he had lived, and I knew the neighborhood very well though I didn't know any of the people he knew. He liked Myron first-rate but Mrs. Ramson got on his nerves. Like most women, she was fussy, and since it was her money that was building the house, what she said had some weight, and the house must have been torn up six times before it was finished, and even when it was finished she wasn't satisfied with the garden gate, but it was impossible to keep from showing off and entertaining any longer. Of course, he was no sooner talking about Mrs. Ramson and telling a priceless story about her giving advice to Myron about driving their first car, when who should appear at the threshold, rather flushed and breathless, but Delia herself?

She was an immense woman and stamped her heels on the floor when she walked, so her sudden appearance was quite a surprise. Barton blushed a little and that was what saved him, for then Delia pretended she'd heard nothing at all but said, "How delightful, Mr. Barton, that you should be meeting Eric in this workman-to workman way! Eric, you know, is the new member of our family, our new butler. How you wild Westerners do meet up with one another without any introductions! But I do hope Eric will learn your beautiful Eastern accent, Mr. Barton, because he has that loud Chicago way of talking you can hear all over the house."

II

SCAROT was the dog. He was a French bull and Mrs. Ramson had bought him as a puppy from a singer in the Metropolitan Opera. This singer must have had a real operatic temperament, or that is the way Mrs. Ramson would explain Scarot's behavior when he ruined someone's new shoes at a tea by biting them viciously. "You see," said Mrs. Ramson, sailing along, "I've thought that when Scarot was a puppy someone kicked him and ever since he has had an aversion for shoes." Most people disliked Scarot and he knew when you disliked him and was very nasty. It was beautiful to see him resting before the fire on the orange tiles of the fireplace, because his body was black and molded like gleaming bronze and he had very quick, pleasant movements. His great indiscretion was chewing pipes - Myron's pipes - for the nicotine in them made him violently sick for three days; he seemed to have no spring in him. Myron left his pipes all over the house, much to the maid's disgust, but Mrs. Ramson tolerated them because she thought pipes were rather masculine and a dignified diversion for a gentleman.

It was fine to see Myron smoke a pipe, for he did do it well and his voice was deep as he talked about Joseph Conrad, and somebody said when he talked that way, smoking, that it was the thundering voice of God from the clouds. He would sit in his study smoking away, reading Rabelais or the newest volume of May Sinclair, and woe to anybody that tried to disturb him then. Mrs. Ramson always became timid when she stood before the door longing to telephone. The telephone was in the study and she would knock very lightly and say sweetly, "Myron?" Sometimes he would answer and sometimes not, but if Mrs. Ramson had made up her mind to telephone she would say again, "Myron?"

"Well," he would answer with just a degree of testiness. "May I telephone?" she would say. "Come in."

She would open the door then and say, "It's just for the grocer, dear."

"I know," he would answer, "but really, my dear, I don't see why you can't telephone in the morning when I'm at the college."

"Now don't be a cross old bear," she would say, patting his hair and adoring him for being cross. He would grunt and settle down deeper in his leather armchair.

Scarot the French bulldog (name in real life: Chicot) who ruined people's new shoes at tea by biting them viciously.

III

I remember the first tea in the house was held in the study. It was several months before the house was finished and we sat on packing boxes. There were no spoons and Myron was elaborately polite: "May I serve you with a splinter, a clean fine splinter of pine wood, to stir your tea with, my dear?" He told me then how in Japan, where they serve chopsticks, the chopsticks are always fresh and this is shown by their not being quite separate, the two being made of one piece of wood. He had been born in China, as his father had been a bishop there, and had lived there until he was fifteen. He had travelled in Japan too, and he was very fond of the East; his love of politeness partly came from his sojourn there, I imagine. Mrs. Ramson respected Myron for all of the Chinese in him, but she was afraid of it too, and one of her strong points was that the "Oriental influence" of the house be limited to the study. There was only one picture in the room, a photograph of the Himalayas, and it concealed a cupboard where some of his manuscripts were kept. Mrs. Ramson always referred to them as the "treasures behind the mountains," and Myron would always brush that remark aside with a deprecating "My dear, my dear," but he was pleased nevertheless. In the beginning he had started out as a poet and short-story writer, but after he married he settled down to teaching. He was fond of mountains and when he couldn't see them he imagined them. I remember one afternoon he was in the Garden Room, which was the room under the drawing room; as the house was built on a hill, the back had an extra storey, and they made it into what they called a Garden Room. Myron held his short-story classes there and it was a very beautiful room. Mrs. Ramson had directed all the "Pompeian influences" in that room, because it was really in the basement and she felt that in a way she had got rid of the Pompeian part of their honeymoon which she detested. Myron was fond of Pompeii and had bought several of the famous bronzes, and Mrs. Ramson had bought the head of Dante in bronze because she hated it but thought that young wives, in the beginning anyway, ought to do what their husbands liked. But now it was a long time since they had been married, and the Pompeian bronzes and the Dante head and most of the old furniture, some of it in Roman style, were relegated to the Garden Room. The walls were of plaster, a rough plaster in light Pompeian red, and the floor was of black and red tiles. The old wicker furniture was repainted a bright green and there were some black pieces too. A pair of French doors led out to the granite-slab terrace, and here it was that Myron was happiest. Just overhead he had hidden a pair of blue electric lights and one red one, and when night came he would turn them on and it would be for all the world like moonlight. "There is a beautiful quality to the stones in the moonlight, don't you think?" he would say, and then be silent for a few moments. The "moonlight" was arranged for the drawing room too, and he was very proud of it. It streamed in a little alcove where white flowers were always placed to catch the ghostly light, and one of the guests would notice that the moon had changed sides that night and then Mrs. Ramson would launch into a description of this lovely idea of Myron's and everybody thought it was very clever.

But I was talking about the mountains. It was an afternoon, a bright spring afternoon, and Myron called me over to the chair where he was sitting and asked me to look at the mountains outside the window. I didn't know what was up, because I knew there were no mountains, but I looked. The windows on the side were long and horizontal, about eight feet long and two feet high, and on a level with the earth which the gardener had just spaded there.

"If you can imagine yourself the height of a fly," said Myron, "you will see that those clods of earth are as beautiful as the picture of the Himalayas in my study."

By half shutting my eyes I could get the effect very well. Myron stayed there the whole afternoon reading and now and again looking at his "mountains." He was reading a book on Einstein, and for days afterward there were conversations on time-sense, and time-place, and relativity, till Mrs. Ramson, who could never stand the rarefied atmosphere of philosophy very long, threatened to outlaw the word "relativity" in the family circle as she had done with the word "reaction." Anybody who used the word "reaction" in the conversation went down ten points in her estimation because she was tired of it and she said it didn't mean anything.

Albert Einstein in 1922, the year this story begins. Professor Ramson read one of his books, but Mrs. Ransom disapproved and threatened to ban the word 'relativity' from her house.

"You naughty psychologists," she said to Professor Marsh at tea, "are just tying up our beautiful language in knots. Every author writing to-day seems to be bathing in psychoses and reactions and psychological moments, until really I wonder if they aren't on a wrong track as far as literature is concerned."

"Now, Mrs. Ramson," said Professor Marsh, who was a large man with a calm way of talking, "don't you be getting psychology and psychoanalysis mixed up; they're quite different things."

"Well, anyway," answered Mrs. Ramson, "that word 'reaction' is not to be used by the friends of Otterby." Later she said she thought Professor Marsh had been rather heavy that day.

But what she really loved to do at tea was to garble a quotation from "Alice in Wonderland" and then turn suddenly on the victim, usually a young instructor whom Professor Ramson was not quite sure of, and say, "Where did that come from?" If he had been warned beforehand, he responded blindly, "Alice in Wonderland," which was always the correct answer, and then Mrs. Ramson would think he was intelligent. If he failed to answer, it was hard for him ever after. Of course, anybody went up ten points if they could garble a quotation cleverly from any work whatsoever. I remember I gave a snapshot of myself to Mrs. Ramson, one of those snapshots that are all high lights and dark shadows, and under it I wrote, "Those were pools that were his eyes," and she said that showed the real literary flair.

There was once a professor who came for a breakfast when they had stewed tomatoes, and Mrs. Ramson thought he was positively pyrotechnic when he recited:

"Gather tomatoes while ye may,
Old time is still a-flying,
And those tomatoes you pluck to-day
To-morrow will be frying."

IV

It was a great honour to be invited to dine with the Ramsons, but to be invited to a Sunday morning breakfast was a special mark of favor. In the summer, breakfasts were held in the Garden Room, but in the winter, in the dining room, where Mrs. Ransom said it was summer all the year. The walls were panelled with vivid wall paper they had bought in Alsace depicting a tropical scene. There were castor-oil plants and orchids and hibiscus and a blue bay and a blue sky, and the ceiling was made to resemble the sky too, light blue plaster with swirls of white and cream. Mrs. Ramson called them "skirls" because they turned around like music. She was very proud of the Scotch blood in the family and used to sing

Scotch songs very off key in the drawing room with Scarot on her lap, and after the second verse he would always join in, wailing in a most unearthly manner. Then Scarot would be extremely proud for the rest of the evening.

Nobody could even touch him after that except perhaps James Stephens. Stephens had a wonderful way with animals; Scarot lost all his dignity before this little man and rolled around the Chinese carpet just to get his attention. Mrs. Ramson had her heart in her mouth all the time Stephens was there because she was afraid Scarot would bite "the precious hands" that had written "The Crock of Gold." The more she warned the author, the more daring he became, tickling Scarot and turning him over, and Scarot squealed and barked till all the guests were thoroughly frightened. You know the way James Stephens is in a drawing room; he's such a tiny man and he is never happy till he is sitting on the floor. He begins at first by sitting properly on the sofa, and then little by little he leans forward and everybody is hypnotized by his Dublin accent - the way he says, "Hooves, the t'umping hooves" - and he leans more and more forward, and gradually he slips farther and farther off the sofa down the sofa leg, and the first thing you know, he is on the floor telling that story about James Joyce. He said that Joyce had invited him into a pub to drink just to tell him that he thought that he was the worst Irish writer that ever was, and then Stephens told Joyce that he thought be was the worst Irish writer in the world, and Mrs. Ramson got very flushed and excited and said "Bravo!" clapping her hands and missing the point of the story altogether, saying that she was sure that that Joyce was not a gentleman, he couldn't be after that terrible bore of "Ulysses."

Stephens stayed three days, talking to all the sparrows around the place in the morning; he was the first great man to visit Otterby, and Robert Frost, who came later, said he had bewitched it, that was what made the house so lovely. Professor Ramson always called Frost "the good gray poet," and the Ramsons were both very fond of him too.

The Irish poet and author James Stephens, who got on well with animals and after staying three days had, according to Robert Frost, "bewitched the house."

V

But I was speaking about the dining room. That it was tropical was to represent their life in Brazil. Mrs. Fife, who lived two doors away in an old farmhouse and who washed dishes and did extra housework sometimes for Mrs. Ramson, told me all about their sojourn there, and lots besides. After their long honeymoon was over, Myron got a position in Rio de Janeiro as a teacher of psychology. He had to teach in Portuguese from a French textbook, and he always recounted that scholastic exploit with deep pleasure. They both adored the life in Rio, where Myron said there were only the very poor and the very rich and a real sense of cosmopolitanism. He still wears a light gray fedora hat with a wide brim suggestive of a sombrero, and he trims his moustache like a Spanish grandee and always takes his hat off with a graceful flourish.

The Professor likes to wear a light grey fedora hat, which he takes off with a graceful flourish.

Mrs. Ramson couldn't stand the climate in Rio, though, so they had to come back to the North, and she spent the next ten years in a chaise longue getting heavier all the time and becoming adept at making dainty sandwiches. She often expressed the opinion that a perfect sandwich was as good as a perfect poem. She still is an invalid, especially when she cares to be, and this gives her a wonderful social lever in the town because she never pays back visits except to Mrs. Heron, the president's wife, and a few other chosen intimates.

The punctiliousness of paying back visits, however, belonged to the next-door neighbour, Mrs. Beebe. She came from Omaha, and Mrs. Ramson got no end of fun watching her antics from the pantry window, but in the end couldn't help liking her because she was so intense and sincere in her ways.

When Professor Beebe brought back this woman from a summer vacation trip, the whole town was agog. Every old maid in the town had given him up as a confirmed bachelor, and everybody said where on earth did he pick up that person? She seemed to be made all of nerves, was small and thin, wearing a brown velvet hat with an immense quill feather on it that stuck out, it seemed in every direction. She wore enormous shell-rimmed glasses, suffered from heart trouble, talked through her nose in a brusque way that used to make Mrs. Ramson squirm, and was forever polishing her windows.

But it was her social tactics that terrified the town. If she invited people to dinner and they didn't pay back their tea call within a week, they were never invited again and she would cut them dead on the street. She also gave musicales, where she broke all the rules of social castes in the town by inviting the head of the history department at the same time as some of the under-librarians and an instructor in the engineering department. The musicales began at eight thirty sharp; Mrs. Beebe crashed the first octave of Rachmaninoff's "Prelude in C Sharp Minor" simultaneously with the striking of the clock, and late guests had to wait until the first group was over. Professor Beebe would wait outside for them and would say, "Don't be sorry that you're late ___ mmm ___" (he had a mannerism of humming suddenly and grinning at the same time) "don't be upset that you're late ___ mmm ___ the best is yet to come ___ mmm ___ Mrs. Beebe is going to render some Debussy ___ some Bartok ___ mmm ___ and Mrs. Marsh is going to sing a new thing ___ mmm ___ of Respighi that she just got through the mail." Then he would laugh. "And, best of all ___ mmm ___ there's Mrs. Beebe's famous chocolate cake and coffee ___ mmm ___ after the musicale!"

He was a hard marker but a popular professor nevertheless because he would give all sorts of intimate details about kings and mistresses that were not in the histories, and his story of Marie Antoinette shivering in the morning as she waited for the sixteenth lady of the bedchamber to hand her her chemise was famous throughout the college.

Mrs. Ramson went to the first musicale out of a burst of abstract neighbourly feeling, but she was an invalid every other time she was invited. She said all she was aware of at the musicale was how the muscles of Mrs. Beebe flexed under the pink tulle sleeves of her evening gown, but that led her to a literary discovery which was a source of tea-table conversation for a whole month.

Professor Beebe's story about Marie Antoinette was famous throughout the college.

VI

"It is incredible," said Mrs. Ramson, "how our great poets make use of muscular impressions in an actual physical way with lips and tongue and lungs; as Keats, in "The Eve of Saint Agnes"; "and lucent syrops tinct with cinnamon" which brings the tongue right to the roof of the mouth with his carefully arranged sibilants so that you seem to be tasting his "syrops' that very minute. And I was exclaiming to Myron only the other day how, in 'The Ride from Ghent to Aix," his "And down on her haunches she shuddered and sank" leaves you as breathless as Browning's tired horse just by exhausting the diaphragm. Isn't it amazing how mechanical some of the purest poetic effects are?"

John Keats used 'carefully arranged sibilants.'

VII

Not long after I had been living in Otterby - indeed, the house was far from finished when we moved in, - one early evening Mrs. Ramson came up to my attic room and knocked at the door. "Are you there, Eric?" she questioned with such a deadly sweetness, I felt my heart sink.

"Come in," I said.

"I hope you're not studying or working," she said; "but even if you are, put it aside for a few minutes, for I want to have just a short heart-to-heart talk with you." She kept smiling all the while as if a heart-to-heart talk was no more serious than at the tea table, and she sat down very deliberately, smoothing out the ruffles of her skirt and crossing her feet. She always wore high buttoned shoes the same as she had worn when she was on her honeymoon, and now they were so démodé she had to have them made specially to order, which she called "a necessary extravagance."

"Now, Eric," she said, "I want you to take seriously what I have to say, but I don't want you to feel hurt, for although you have many faults you are young still and have a chance to correct them.

"Now, you simply must learn to speak more quietly and drop your r's a little more, because neither Myron nor I can tolerate this abominable Chicago accent. It does seem a pity that people of quality are born in such places, but the fact remains that you are, and you must learn to hide it. Now, another thing that might lead people with less perception than we have, to think you were not a gentleman is that you don't wipe your feet sufficiently on coming into the house, and you know our good workmen are becoming more and more fretful every day because there are dirty marks on the newly varnished floor. You must watch Myron Ramson; there's a gentleman for you, a noble example: he always wipes his feet thoroughly on the mat outside, sometimes for a whole minute." "Yes," I replied politely.

She got up in a great flurry of emotion as if she wished to say more but had decided not to, unexpectedly kissing me on the forehead. "You're a dear boy," she said, and rushed out of the room.

I did not go down to supper, as I was not feeling well. The change of food had kept me unwell for the three days previous, and rather late in the evening Myron came up to see me.

"I hope I'm not bothering you, Eric," he said, "but I've just unpacked a treasure and I thought you might like to see it."

I followed him downstairs to the study, and the house was still, as Mrs. Ramson had already gone to bed.

The "treasure" stood on the window sill at the far end of the book-lined corridor of the study, and gleamed softly in the light. It was a delicate replica of the Taj Mahal in alabaster, and the dark floor gave the illusion of water in a long pool in front. I was delighted with the lacy carving of the minarets and the translucency of the stone.

"I like the quality of the light very much, don't you?" said Myron. "This temple was a gift to Bishop Ramson from some of his Hindu converts, for you know he was in India before he went to China."

A little later the conversation shifted and Myron said, looking at me very kindly, "We mustn't mind these womenfolk too much, you know; they're often more impulsive than they mean."

The treasure stood on the window sill and gleamed softly in the light.

VIII

The kitchen was Mrs. Ramson's particular triumph. It was in orchid and pale green, with a breakfast nook, a pantry directly connecting, and an electric stove. The pantry was just big enough for Mrs. Ramson and no one else; she sat on a revolving chair placed in the middle of the floor with her work table before and the ice box behind. All the ladies who visited the kitchen were charmed with this arrangement, and Mrs. Ramson turned around and around in the chair to show how practical it was. Mrs. Jayson, one of the younger wives of the faculty, said about Mrs. Ramson that "for a lady without a thyroid she did very well." Delia had to take sheep-thyroid pills every day and she always tried to keep it a secret.

For a while the electric stove was the greatest bother. It was off when it was supposed to be on, on when off, and forever putting the house in darkness by blowing the fuse. It also heated in an erratic fashion; for a long while it would not heat at all, and then the plate would become so hot that everything would burn, and as the plates didn't change colour with the heat, more than once you burned yourself. But the worst was that the stove would be left on all night consuming watts and watts of electricity, and always one of the plates would be ruined and the electrician would have to be called in. Once Mrs. Ramson left a chicken in the oven which burned to a cinder, and the smoke that rolled out of the oven when she opened it blackened the orchid ceiling and it was an awful job to clean.

Mrs. Ramson was getting desperate about the stove. The prestige of owning the only electric stove in the town was certainly dearly paid for. And then Professor Marsh of the psychology department saved the situation by explaining auditory memory to her. Auditory memory was simply saying, as you turned off the stove, "Out, out, out, out, out, out, out," for every one of the seven dials, and then in bed, when you wondered whether the stove was still going on or not, your voice would come floating up the stairs of your memory, "Out, out, out, out, out, out, out."

IX

Myron had his hand in the breakfast nook, which was made like an old-fashioned church pew. He cut little openings in the sides with a fret saw in the design of a fleur-de-lis and then lined the fleur-de-lis with red paint, and they were very gay. Radiators were placed out of sight under the seats, so that they were always warm in winter, sometimes too warm, and guests would squirm and wonder where on earth all the heat was coming from.

Myron also did some varnishing of the oak timbers on the outside of the house, for he had a Ruskin feeling that he must contribute to the labour of his dwelling, and Delia said that Myron's contribution was the best of all because it was done in a "spirit of pure craftsmanship" and the timbers he had varnished gave a "lift" to the house that it would not have had otherwise.

Myron was really happy puttering around with the workmen, and they didn't mind because he let them do what they pleased. He listened very carefully to their conversation to get "the interesting American speech rhythms," and he said their language was very vivid. He liked to recount at dinner how one of them had said, "I hit a nail where it wasn't."

"The precision of that!" exclaimed Myron with admiration. "It has such a virile impact."

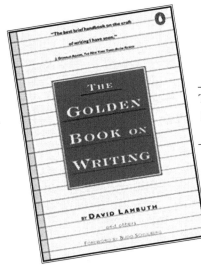

The real "Professor Ramson's", i.e. Professor David Lambuth's, book in which he stresses the need for precision in writing.

X

Saturday was the biggest day of the week for Mrs. Ramson because invariably it meant a big dinner in the evening. If the guest was to be a great man, preparations would begin on Friday.

First there would be the telephoning. "Is Mr. Chaffee there? I want to speak to Mr. Chaffee personally. It is Mrs. Ramson speaking."

The men at Chaffee's simply fled when Mrs. Ramson occasionally visited them, which was usually when she went to the movies. She adored Rudolf Valentino. "Myron," she would say, "his face has the real medieval contour; it's not a modern face at all." Even Myron went to see "Monsieur Beaucaire," and then there were disquisitions for a whole week on the art of Booth Tarkington. "Tarkington," said Myron, "is a beautiful example of the man who almost makes it, but not quite. I must confess there is something that gets me in "Monsieur Beaucaire.' 'Seventeen' is an extraordinary achievement for an American, but "The Magnificent Ambersons' goes no farther than his first books, which was just not quite far enough."

"Mr. Chaffee?" continued Mrs. Ramson; "now, you know I'm going to have a great splendid dinner to-night, and I know you're going to help me make it a success, aren't you, Mr. Chaffee?

"Now, I want three heads of lettuce, the real firm, Mrs. Ramson kind that I can cut in little pieces so the guests won't have to use their knives, and bread, and two pounds of butter.

"How many loaves? Two, as usual, and you'll be sure that they're fresh piping hot, won't you? The last bread was a little, just a little…"

By the time the telephoning was done, the florist would have delivered the flowers, and the rest of the morning would be spent in arranging them. Delia was really very skillful at this, and sometimes, as a special favour to a new bride in the community, she would invite her on Saturday morning to explain the art of flower arranging.

"Something wonderful happens to flowers when they catch the light," Mrs. Ramson would say, moving one of the electric lamps so that the rays would fall directly into the red cup of a tulip. The drawing room was elaborately equipped with lamp plugs so that the lamps could be moved all over the room easily. There were many candles too, and little tables where the flat green Chinese platters of flowers, usually violets or daisies, showed up very well.

The next step in the ceremony was the setting of the table. Mrs. Ramson would open the dining room cupboards and bring out all the iridescent goblets and polish them, and then the heavy green faïence plates she had bought in Italy with bouillon cups to match, and all the fine Sèvres plates for the pièce de résistance, and the brilliant Chinese red salad plates and the crystal sherbert glasses and the dainty Delft demitasses–oh, but she was proud of her china!

The cupboards were the idea of Mrs. Ramson; they were painted Chinese red inside, and then she dappled them herself with gold, so they made a brilliant setting indeed. When the table was finally set with its immaculate linen, and gleaming silver, and goblets, and pink roses in the centre, and the heavy silver candlesticks, it was a pretty sight.

In the afternoon Mrs. Ramson would rest before tea, and the tea would be very simple. Guests that showed an inclination to stay were gently shooed out with a remark like: "We're so looking forward to meeting Colonel Steinlich tonight at dinner," or, "How the snow deceives one! It keeps the day so light you think it is much earlier than it actually is," or, in desperate cases, "Your conversation is so charming I do hope you'll be coming to see us soon again." This Colonel Steinlich was a town character. President Heron saw him wandering around the Austrian Embassy at Washington and, finding out that he was in need of a job, hired him on the spot to be the fencing and skiing instructor.

He was a tall man with a deep voice, he always clicked his heels together when he bowed, and caused a sensation in Mrs. Jayson's drawing room by kissing her hand on departure. His English was far from perfect, but he could swear impeccably and did so volubly at the ski jump. The American student, with his irresponsibility and sudden enthusiasms, always remained a mystery to him.

When he first began teaching fencing, he was very contemptuous of his American students and fenced with them, sometimes two or three of them at a time without a guard. He suffered from his attitude, though, for at the end of the first week the American captain got him, and the poor Colonel had to stay in the hospital for quite a while.

The hospital was an amazing building. It was made of bilious yellow brick with huge granite urns at the doorway, and built in perfect Mansard style in the form of a sprawling cross with low arches all around the place. But the nurses were pleasant.

Nobody knew about the Colonel for a long time, and then he suddenly leaped into prominence by one of his remarks. He was conducting a special ski class for the faculty, and as it was in the morning the class was made up mostly of the wives, the college chaplain, and the ministers of the town. When little Mrs.

Soccy fell down, the chaplain rushed to assist her, but Colonel Steinlich was just as quick in preventing him. "Eef you help up a lady," he said, "all zee ladies will be falling down."

Note: The real name of Imbs's Colonel 'Steinlich' was Colonel Dietrich.

President Ernest Martin Hopkins of Dartmouth ("President Heron" in the novel). He saw Colonel Steinlich "wandering around the Austrian Embassy" and hired him to be a ski and fencing instructor.

XI

After the last tea guest had departed, Mrs. Ramson slipped on an apron and began the cooking in earnest, while I dressed, being the butler. I never could tie my bow tie and would finally go down to the kitchen all dressed but for that.

"Now, my Admirable Crichton," (she had given me the book as an object lesson in butlering) Delia would say, tying my bow tenderly - it always gave her a motherly feeling to do so - "we're going to have a wonderful dinner, perfectly served, aren't we?"

"Yes," I would say. "Have you brought down the wine?"

She never had, so I would dash up to the attic, where the bottles were romantically hidden in case Federal agents ever should raid Otterby.

Hidden in the attic because of Prohibition.

XII

The attic was a queer place. It was piled high with suitcases and trunks heavily belabelled with the names of foreign cities and famous hotels. All the books that Myron had discarded from the study were there too, and represented his psychological-sociological period. There were strange Arabian books on the perversities of sex, books on birth control, books on the protective tariff, and a heap of war books which still retained their flaming covers.

One of the trunks belonged to Roger Fadden Mote, who translated Ronsard and Japanese poetry. He left college when I came, just to devote all his time to the tiny haikus.

"If only silent they would go,
The herons flying across the sky
Were but a line of snow."

When the first snow of the winter came, Myron and Delia rushed out bareheaded to see how Otterby would look against the white hills in the distance. They were surprised how the roof, which was painted green, stood out. Of all the parts of the house, the workmen disliked the roof most; it was painted in three shades of green, in three horizontal stripes, the lightest shade being the rooftree, and this also added to the "lift" of the house.

But I was talking about Colonel Steinlich's dinner. By the time I had come down to the kitchen with the wine, it would be ready to toast the round pieces of bread for the caviar. Both the Ramsons liked hors d'oeuvres so much that they always served it at their dinners, contrary to all rules.

"Now," said Delia, "watch these canapés" (the little circles of toast were called canapés). "They must not be brown put pale yellow, and only on one side; otherwise it makes it hard for the guest to cut them. The hostess must always think of the comfort of her guests." She would be all ready here to go into a long disquisition on the finer points of entertaining, when the peas would begin to burn or the potatoes to bubble over, and after she had tended them the subject would be forgotten.

"Now," said Delila, "watch these canapés."

Then, when everything was going nicely, the caviar had been spread on the toasts, the celery arranged on the plates with the butter and tomatoes, the roast was in the oven, and all was right with the world, Mrs. Ramson would go upstairs to dress.

Dressing for the evening was usually a hectic performance for her, and when there was a big dinner on, like the one for Rebecca West, she would have Mrs. Fife to help her. Once, Mrs. Fife said, she was in an awful hurry (she always stayed down in the kitchen too long, but she felt that everything would go wrong otherwise) and when finally she got into her evening gown, which was rather décolleté - she had beautiful white skin – she discovered to her horror that some of the lingerie showed. Without stopping a moment, Mrs. Fife said, she seized the scissors and cut off all the lingerie that showed, thus ruining the best she had. Mrs. Fife admired her very much for this, but she was getting so that she could no longer stand Mrs. Ramson's fussiness. "When she first came to the university she wasn't like that," said Mrs. Fife, "but as people get older they get set in their ways."

Mrs. Fife wasn't so young herself, but she always worked hard and kept a kind of youthful vigour. She had the pleasant habit of making doughnuts on the cold winter mornings, and if I passed by I cleaned her walkway of snow and got a few. They were the real New England product, flaky and light and not greasy.

Mrs. Ramson always pronounced the word greasy "greazy". She had a horror of her china being washed in water that was "all greazy," and would change the water after every four pieces. This process, which made dishwashing a dilettante occupation, was all right when one had all the afternoon and only the breakfast dishes, but to clean up the dozens of plates and saucers and cups after a big dinner was another matter. Mrs. Ramson wouldn't trust Marie, the Indian maid, not to break them, and she wouldn't trust me to follow out her process exactly. I didn't wash dishes very well anyway.

I remember the first time I washed dishes there it was in the early evening and the Ramsons were away. When they returned I conversed a little with them and said there had been a pleasant sunset. But at the end of the week, when I showed the extra hours I had worked, Mrs. Ramson was sure I had been wasting her time watching sunsets, and I was never able to convince her to the contrary.

So after a big dinner Mrs. Fife would come early the next morning at five AM, and the dishes would be beautifully washed, and Mrs. Ramson would ask Mrs. Fife if she had used her system of changing the hot water after every four pieces so that the water wasn't "all greazy," and Mrs. Fife always said "Yes," to ease Mrs. Ramson's conscience, but she really never did; "tomfool notion" was what she called it.

XIII

The first guest to arrive was the Colonel and he was not in evening clothes. For a stranger in the town, the question of evening clothes was an irritating one. Some of the professorial households held that a dinner coat was only snobbish, a bother, and an extra expense, and if a guest arrived wearing one he felt uncomfortable the entire evening. On the other hand, the more formal and dignified professors like Professor Ramson kept to the tradition, and when a guest arrived in an ordinary sack coat it was an unpleasant faux pas.

Sometimes the young worried instructors who had been invited - and those dinners were always in the nature of a social test - would telephone to ask whether the dinner was formal or not, and Mrs. Ramson would always answer, "Why, yes, of course," in such a way that the young instructors at the other end must have withered. Mrs. Ramson could be very catty over the telephone, and when Myron (who otherwise would have reproached her) was away she would call up all the people who lived on Cedar Ridge, across the pond, after ten o'clock because she knew they were then in bed. Almost the whole biology department lived over there, and as they did not contribute much to the social life Mrs. Ramson did not think much of them. She also had a grudge against Cedar Ridge because she had wanted to live there. It was really the best site in the town, but some little chemistry professor without any social aims at all had snapped up the last available piece of property, so one of Mrs. Ramson's cherished dreams went up in thin air. When someone referred to the fact of their location, Mrs. Ramson would say, "Of course, at first, when we couldn't settle on the Ridge, I was broken-hearted, but now I'm really much more satisfied where I am; we have the hills instead of the sky for a background." It was sour grapes, nevertheless.

So, with all this feeling behind her, Mrs. Ramson would begin telephoning: "Oh, I'm so sorry, I had no idea I was bringing you out of bed. It's only ten, you know. Myron Ramson never goes to bed before two, and usually four, so I simply can't get used to the rustic habits of you people on the Ridge. - Oh, no, it was nothing important; I'm all alone and was just wanting a little chat. So sorry I've disturbed you. Good-bye, sleep well." She would be in good humour the rest of the evening.

But I was talking about Colonel Steinlich arriving in an ordinary sack suit because the week before he had gone to a dinner in the other circle of the town in evening clothes, thus making an error, and now here he was making an error again. He saw Myron behind me, who had just descended in all the magnificence of full dress, and in confusion he said to me, "I go back; I come back soon dressed grand."

I relaxed the cold butler face I put on for such occasions, and told him to come out of the cold, and that it was no matter. And Myron, seeing there was something wrong, stepped forth and invited him too, so there was no retreat for him.

"You see, Colonel Steinlich," said Myron, not pompous, but very conscious he was correctly attired, "handsome men like you have no need of special clothes, but old, wrinkled professors like me depend a great deal on our dress."

They went into the drawing room then, Professor Ramson looking particularly splendid, as he wore his nose glasses with a long black ribbon; ordinarily he wore a pair of pince-nez, but for the evening he wore the others, which were much more professorial. The other guests soon arrived, Mr. and Mrs. Moorhead.

Mr. Moorhead was a young instructor in the English department who was popular enough with the students and who delighted Mrs. Ramson's heart, as one side of his face resembled Savonarola, the other a real Virginia gentleman, while the front elevation was almost straight Emerson, all of these being favourite heroes of hers. He was a little man, charming in his speech. He had never been farther than Harvard in his travels, and he sat almost always with one leg under him, clasping his long ivory cigarette holder with both hands as if it were a mug. He held a short-story class on Tuesday nights at his house, or rather his half house, for Nadia Schultz Rosenkrantz and her husband occupied the other half, and his wife came into the affectionate regard of the students, as more than once she served coffee and cake, and once even strawberry ice cream. She was a tall, reserved woman, but I soon found out that in order to preserve her liberty of thought and action in that gossipy town she had to maintain her detachment. She was very cordial to me always, and though the butler part of me was revolted at such intimacy with a guest, the human part of me rather exulted in it.

In the drawing room, with its glowing flowers, softly lit by candles on high brass candlesticks, and the crackling wood fire gleaming again in the orange tiles, the party waited for Mrs. Ramson. There would be moments of silence, for conversation was always difficult in the beginning, and always at such moments would be heard the slamming of drawers overhead, for the walls of the house were thin. An exquisite shade of annoyance would pass over Myron's face at such moments, and he would lean forward and tell another story quickly.

I was always in the hall waiting outside the drawing room, and suddenly Mrs. Ramson would appear on the landing above, dressed in black velvet, generously cut with trimmings of fur about the skirt. She would pause at the landing, breathless from exertion, her hair curling about her face in that careful-careless manner which took so much time to arrange but which was so youthful and Virginian; and, taking a long breath for the evening, she descended the stairs like a catastrophe. She rushed out to the kitchen before going into greet her guests, and then would say to me, "The ice is in the glasses, you have your water, don't forget to bring the chicken in straight to Mr. Ramson to carve, yes, there's the wine. Oh, the candles aren't lit … no, don't light them till I come in, they're so expensive anyway."

Then she would go to the door. "Do I look all right?" she would ask me.

"Beautiful, as always," I would answer, opening the doors to the drawing room.

Her entrance was a signal for a general upset, and she had a genius for arriving when everyone was in the midst of a phrase. "Oh, sit down, sit down, don't bother about me," she would say in that gay-lady manner, crossing the room in a series of billows to Mrs. Moorhead. "How are you, my dear? I'm so glad you've come." Then she would sit down and I had to listen carefully at the door, for the interval between Mrs. Ramson's entrance and my announcement of dinner was a nice one; I would receive a kind of thought wave from her finally, and then I opened the doors abruptly, but not too abruptly, and took one step into the room, and, staring at the window in front of me, I would announce pretentiously, but not too pretentiously, in my best Eastern accent, "Dinner is served."

Then, as I took my post at the doorway, glacial and immobile, there would be a general scramble for partners. Mrs. Ramson never had half women and half men at a party, because one of her entertaining principles was that a woman was equal to two men in the amount of conversation they did. At this dinner the ratio was two to three, but it generally was two to four, and sometimes two to five. The latter ratio was for celebrated women, because they always talked twice as much as an ordinary woman. "You must expect that a celebrated woman will glitter," Delia would say.

Then the party would file past me, Mrs. Ramson in high spirits just at anticipating the wine and thinking of Colonel Steinlich, who was enjoying a real chic at the moment – the President knew he would be good advertising for the college - and who must have turned down three dinner engagements in favour of the one he had accepted. But then Mrs. Ramson had a high reputation as a cook in the town, and though the dinners were always the same - Myron and Delia had evolved a perfect dinner and scarcely ever varied it: hors d'œuvres, consommé, Japanese baked crab, roast chicken, potatoes, lettuce salad, and a lemon sherbert - there was always plenty to eat, which was quite extraordinary among professorial households.

As soon as they had passed me, I would rush into the drawing room and blow out all the candles and add a log to the fire. When I returned to the dining room, the guests would have been all comfortably seated and Mrs. Ramson would exclaim, "Oh, the candles! I forgot to light the candles! Now the hostess has made a terrible mistake and everyone can be at their ease." Then I would light the candles, already a little angry that a dinner had to start out on a left foot to be right according to Mrs. Ramson's notions. Of course, everyone felt ill at ease for the rest of the dinner, especially as most of the guests were not accustomed to the elaborate service of a butler, and table rules differed in almost every household. Mrs. Ramson wanted two butlers, but Myron put his foot down on that. He said it would be "putting on side."

Of course, Mrs. Ramson's gaucherie was also the springboard needed for Myron's favourite small talk, the etiquette books which were at that moment enjoying a great vogue in America. He would recount gleefully the questions he could not answer: "Where should the owner of the car sit when someone else is driving?" or "What guests should a hostess serve tea to first--the ones nearest or farthest away?" When Myron got started talking, usually he did not stop, and often he held up a course - generally the dessert course - and Mrs. Ramson would tell him "hurry up" in Portuguese and then begin talking about Brazil in an effort to shut him off. I learned soon enough that there was no taking away the plate from Myron until he had finished; he would say, quite audibly, "Not yet, please."

That was not like Swinnerton, that famous English writer, when he visited the Ramsons and dined with them; he took no chances but held on to his knife and fork, one in each fist, as he stopped eating to talk, because in England the plate is taken away the moment the knife and fork are laid down. Swinnerton never had a college education, and Mrs. Ramson said the lack of it really didn't show. The only thing she had against Swinnerton, or rather the only thing she could not get reconciled to, was his deep admiration for Arnold Bennett.

"Bennett," said Swinnerton, "is the only man who can talk about God at the dinner table and have people take him seriously." Mrs. Ramson answered that she thought that sounded rather "bumptious," and really, if a man wrote such dreadful books, he must be a rather terrible person. She was referring to the fact that his books reminded her of unpleasant things, and that was a cardinal sin in the Ramson family, since life was difficult enough!

Frank Swinnerton. He held onto his knife and fork, one in each fist, as he stopped eating to talk.

Delia even refused to read Conrad because she said he wrote for men; occasionally Myron would read aloud from "The Nigger of the Narcissus," which he liked very much, and his deep voice would resound in the room, giving Jane and Mrs. Ramson the shivers. Delia would only tolerate it once in a great while. The strain on the emotions was too great. It was the same way after Robert Frost had left Otterby after a visit of three days; Delia said that living on his high plane was too exhausting for ordinary folk, and the whole family would go in for relaxation, even Myron taking a nap before his luncheon and in the afternoon. Alas, Myron was reaching the nadir of his vitality again; he never believed in taking exercise, and always ate what pleased him in plenty until he got really run down. Then he would take a leave of absence for a year and go to Paris or the Bahamas to rest up, and always returned more fit than he had ever been. He always took these trips alone and travelled first class, for Mrs. Ramson said that was the only natural way for a grand seigneur to go. In Paris he never smoked his cigars, in order not to be taken for an American, but rather wishing to be seen as a Brazilian gentleman of a great plantation, and he talked Portuguese a good deal. In England he was always taken for an Englishman, as he only had to broaden his accent the slightest bit to make it pure Oxford. When he went travelling, Mrs. Ramson always referred to him as "the greatest man in the world". She really thought that Myron and Roger Fadden Mote were the greatest men in the world-and in June, when Myron really had a lot of work to do and saw ever so many students and kept getting more and more nervous by keeping up his even degree of constant courtesy, Mrs. Ramson said that the students were "crucifying Mr. Ramson."

But I was talking about this dinner for Colonel Steinlich. The Colonel that evening was not given to talk, and replied very succinctly to all the leading questions Mrs. Ramson started. She began once in a general way about skiing.

"Skiing," said the Colonel, "ees a matter of stomach nerves. Zhe stronger zhey are, ze more farzer can you chump"; and that was all. I think he was angry about the wine, for he took a good big drink in the beginning and then drank only water afterwards. Nobody who really liked wine liked the product Mrs. Ramson made except an elderberry wine which she served very rarely. When the wine was made in the autumn, something always went wrong: there was too much yeast or not enough, the grapes were not good or they weren't ripe enough, or the wine was strained too much or not enough - anyway, something always went wrong, but Mrs. Ramson always discovered a virtue in it and got very gay at dinner and flushed, and breathed rapidly.

Mrs. Moorhead said nothing at the table at all except how delicious everything was, especially the sherbert. That was enough to endear her to Mrs. Ramson, for the sherbert was Mrs. Ramson's own invention and there was no getting around it, it was good. But she was terribly fussy in making it. I had to cut the ice just so; if there had been a way to cut the ice in cubes she would have liked that better; I had to make a prayer when I put the salt in the ice, for once a little salt got into the fruit juice and ruined the sherbert, and the whole next week I was reminded that people who couldn't make a sherbert wouldn't turn out to be anything much anyway, because the faculty of following directions was the most important one in carving out a success in life. After she had put the fruit juice in made of lemon and oranges and a little lemon peel, and there was an unholy amount of grinding to be done. Then, when it had been made and served, always in season with a spray of mint or a candied rosebud, I had what was left on the little wooden paddles to myself, and it seemed to me that that was the best part of the sherbert. I always had to eat it quickly, for they would be ready for coffee in the drawing room almost immediately; besides, I had to chase out to the drawing room around outside and enter by the side door, so that the guests wouldn't see me, to relight the candles and add a log to the fire.

The coffee urn was a great rosy copper one, and it always trembled on its pins when I carried it into the drawing room, the alcohol burner underneath flaring like mad. Mrs. Ramson got so intense on watching it, for she was sure I would stumble and spill it all over the expensive Chinese rug - the kind Myron had rolled upon as a bab, Mrs. Ramson said - for she had had one beautiful rug spoiled by students who had just come off the oiled road and left tracks all over; she got so intense just watching it that she hypnotized me almost and I had visions of standing frozen for eternity holding a flaming coffee urn. All the guests in the room sensed the danger that was abroad, and stopped talking and watched me in the silence. The worst thing was the two steps I had to descend in going into the room, for I could not see my feet and there was no railing to guide me. Myron always descended them like a king stepping off his throne; but Mrs. Ramson was never sure of them, as there was a dark line running through the middle of the grain of one of them that looked like the edge but wasn't. "Don't forget the stairs," she would remind the guests. Delia and Myron had really intended having an iron railing in a Spanish pattern, but the cost was so prohibitive, and it came as a last item, that Mrs. Ramson cut it off, at least for ten years.

Well, I never once fell with that coffee urn, but it was really too much one evening when Mrs. Ramson said the coffee wasn't strong enough and I had to take it back to the kitchen and return with it the same evening five minutes later. I breathed a sigh of relief when it was finally deposited at the little table by Mrs. Ramson where the little Chinese idol was. The little idol was a malicious-looking thing with only half an arm. It was a real one given to her husband's father Bishop Ramson, and Mrs. Ramson liked it because she said so many prayers had been made to it that it had become really scornful. The idol was beautifully carved and it did seem to have a nasty spirit in it. I always felt triumphant when I put the urn down beside it, and it always seemed furious.

Then would ensue the how-many-lumps-and do-you-take-cream period. Mrs. Ramson would always ask Myron in Portuguese - "Simplis ou com lache?" - as he always changed his mind from one dinner to another. After the coffee he would smoke a white meerschaum pipe. (Delia insisted on an appropriate pipe for evening wear.) And then he would begin talking on one of his favourite subjects, namely his book on "Creative Criticism" that was begun but never finished because he was always changing his ideas and he never seemed to have the time. The first chapter began, "Much ink has been spilled on the question, What is art?..."

Delia's special sherberts were decorated with candied rosebuds in winter and spring, or with sprigs of mint in summer and autumn.

XIV

I remember very well the afternoon I typed one of the chapters of "Creative Criticism." I sat at a little table in the Garden Room at the machine ready for dictation while Myron sat in one of the great green wicker chairs filling his pipe. It was an immense calabash he had bought in Germany, and it curved as low as his chest. The colour was beautiful, a rich amber shading to pale yellow and white at the edge of the cup. Soon clouds of smoke were pouring out, wreathing his bearded face so that he looked like a legendary hero.

The chapter was on Conrad, and Myron began calmly and resonantly:

"The outstanding quality of this great modern writer is the synthesis he has achieved of the calm, brooding, meditative Slav temperament with the precise, concrete, suggestive English tongue and the characteristic English love of action." As the dictation progressed Myron became more and more excited and paced the room, while I typed faster and faster on the machine. Smoke filled the Garden Room. He kept repeating and repeating the same ideas, getting more and more involved in his grammar and making regular Henry James periods. Finally he stopped abruptly. "That is all. What do you think of it?"

"It seems to me rather turgid toward the end," I said.

"Well, naturally, naturally," said Myron, a little nettled; "I shall polish it up this evening."

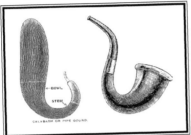

Myron smoked a green calabash pipe.

XV

The evening, on the whole, was not a brilliant one. Colonel Steinlich once got started about Austrian mountain lodges, but Mrs. Ramson could not resist breaking in and telling about an exciting mountain adventure she had had near Grenoble, and the Colonel, being interrupted, became moody and stared at the fire the rest of the evening. Delia and two other girls were climbing the mountains when suddenly a storm broke. "There we were," said Delia, "in the midst of those frowning mountains, far from our *pension*. The rain began falling heavily, the lightning flashed, and the thunder echoed in the mountains in a terrifying way. Luckily one of the girls, I think it was myself, espied a light in the window of a mountaineer's cottage not far distant. We hastened to it, and the two old French peasants took us in, and they were charming, and the old lady taught me how to make a peasant soup which is really delicious and, in the good French manner, costs next to nothing. Just water and onions, seasoning, and lots of bread. You boil the bread right with the soup, and it expands and expands and expands and takes up a lot of room in the 'tummy', doesn't it, Myron?"

Myron, who had not been listening, replied absent-mindedly, "Yes," and then continued talking to Mr. Moorhead about Sherwood Anderson. "I must confess," said Myron, "that for all his unpleasant preoccupation with sex the man does not write badly."

Mr. Moorhead, who was a young man and sympathetic to the moderns, said that he had always thought Mrs. Edith Wharton was the greatest writer in America but after reading "The Triumph of the Egg" he thought that Anderson was more deserving of the title. "Oh," said Myron, "it's difficult to say."

"Anderson has a very clear and vivid way of presenting the mind of his characters," said Mr. Moorhead.

Sherwood Anderson irritated Professor Ramson because "the minds he presents are always cracked minds".

"Yes, but what irritates me," answered Myron, "is that the minds he presents are always cracked minds. Now, you take Conrad; he never forgets the sublimity of the human being; even 'The Nigger of the Narcissus' has a certain divinity to it."

"But at least," said Mr. Moorhead, "you will admit that technically he is much in advance of that writer the reviews are praising so highly, Dreiser."

"Oh, Dreiser!" broke in Mrs. Ramson scornfully; "Dreiser, that blunderbuss!" She was tiring of the domestic conversation with Mrs. Moorhead, and later she said thank goodness that Mrs. Moorhead wasn't one of those dreadful intellectuals.

"I find his style very lumbering," said Myron.

"He must be an impossible person as well as an impossible writer," continued Delia. "I was talking only a week ago with a woman who entertained him at luncheon, Mrs. Smythe, you know, the wife of that dear old man who was editor of the Century so long. She said when she announced luncheon to Dreiser he replied, 'Well, I hope it will be good,' and then he ate like a bear."

"Well, my dear," said Myron deprecatingly, "you can't make literary judgments on a man's social behaviour."

"Oh, yes, you can," said Delia very positively; "a woman can, I mean; she has her intuition."

Myron smiled tiredly, for he did not like to have his wife interrupt his gentle cross examination of Mr. Moorhead. "What would you women do without it?" he asked ironically.

The party broke up shortly afterwards and everybody began talking volubly in the hall. Even the Colonel began to expand in the warm, bright light and clicked his heels loudly as he bowed. The hall was plastered light green with a special weave kind of texture. And then, as there was so much gold paint left, Delia got one of her happy intuitions and, while the plaster was still wet, mashed the paint into a powder and then blew the powder into the plaster by means of a piece of macaroni. The gold, so thinly sprinkled on the walls, was not visible except when the light struck it, and then it gleamed but softly, making the hall seem very rich and gay. There was a wall vase of copper filled with flowers. And in that bit of wall which was just under the landing of the stairs was a little niche, the inside painted a dull blue-green which served as a background for a priceless piece of antique Oriental pottery, a Satsuma bowl, which a Japanese prince had presented to Bishop Ramson. The bowl was pale green, almost white, with a cover, delicately decorated with painted flowers. Above the niche swung a pale yellow Venetian lamp, a long cylinder of light, and Mrs. Ramson said the niche was the "heart of the house."

When the guests had finally left, Myron bolted the great arched English door that led into the hall, first making sure that Scarot, who always slipped out while the guests were saying good-by, had entered. The house always seemed very empty just after the guests had left, and the dining room, with the stained goblets standing about, looked quite desolate. The kitchen was always a picture of confusion, because I always had my hands full just with serving and looking out for the meat and dishing out the sherbert to be paying much attention to the symmetrical arrangement of dirty plates and saucers.

Mrs. Ramson would always try to break the heavy atmosphere by being impossibly gay all in a spurt and dancing into the drawing room from the kitchen, where she had been foraging, now with a chicken bone, now with a plate of cold Japanese baked crab that someone didn't eat, and she would call to Myron, who was fixing the fire for the night, "Oh, Myron, aren't you hungry, dear? Come on out to the kitchen and have a bite."

He would follow her out to the kitchen a moment later, while she bustled around clattering dishes and piling them pell-mell all over to make a place in the breakfast nook. She always liked to have something in her mouth; at odd moments of the day she chewed pieces of straw which she plucked nervously from the broom. This always disgusted Myron, who would say, "My dear, how can you! It's been all over the floor!"

Then they would sit down to eat, finishing up the chicken and the crab and the salad, and Mrs. Ramson would make a fresh cup of coffee - Java Express, and it was good-and invite me to join them. "I must say," Myron would begin, smiling, "that the dinner was most exquisitely served, as fine as in the great restaurants," and Mrs. Ramson would beam at me, forgetting for the moment that I had totally forgotten to serve the Camembert with the salad and had to be reminded it was in the ice box and that the crackers were just above the molasses on the top shelf in the bright tin box. They would be sitting together then discussing the dinner and the guests until two and three in the morning, the lights blazing all over the house - "lit up like a church," Mrs. Fife said - so that any stray nocturnal traveller would know that one family in the town, at any rate, kept sophisticated hours.

Delia would often pull straws out of a broom and chew them because she always had to have something in her mouth.

XVI

NADIA SCHULTZ ROSENKRANTZ returned from Russia with her husband and a tablecloth of the Czar. Mrs. Ramson said the linen was not of extraordinary quality, but she was jealous because she thought the greatest man in the world should be eating off of it rather than a little mathematics professor who played the viola. Still, Mrs. Ramson liked Nadia very much because she was "picturesque", and Nadia always talked about Mrs. Ramson, who was so "original" and lived in such an "original" house. When Nadia came to tea Mrs. Ramson always invited her on condition that she wear her national costume, and Nadia was always more or less uncomfortable with those rattling wooden beads around her neck, but Mrs. Ramson said it was "so sweet" and added "such colour" to the drawing room.

Nadia was a medium-sized woman with very black hair severely parted in the middle and falling loosely over her ears in two great waves. She wore heavy shell-rimmed glasses, and her eyes were so intense and piercing that she could hypnotize people with them, and then she bathed them in a flood of sentimental small talk about the Imperial Family of Russia, so that Myron, who simply could not retire when once he was in her grip, used to suffer visibly and was never to be found in the house if he got an inkling that "that Russian woman" had been invited.

Delia adored the photo of Robert Louis Stevenson with the silky, droopy moustaches, and a velvet coat.

Her favourite book was "Thelma: A Norwegian Princess"; the Norwegians were so "original," she said, and she tried to convert Mrs. Ramson to its author Marie Corelli, but without success. In the matter of books Mrs. Ramson differed from Myron only in two things: she thought Barrie was greater than Shakespeare and that Robert Louis Stevenson, despite certain youthful indiscretions, was one of the few real gentlemen who had ever lived and who was a great writer at the same time. Myron would always snort at Stevenson; "boudoir literature" he called it. What really got on his nerves was the sedulous ape part of Stevenson. "That is no way to write," said Myron; "you must follow the 'intuition,' as Croce calls it, write rapidly until the 'intuition' is exhausted, and correct afterwards." But Mrs. Ramson read R. L. S. faithfully, and adored that picture of him with the silky, droopy moustaches and a velvet coat. When Swinnerton came - you know, he wrote "Robert Louis Stevenson: A Critical Study" - she talked a long time with him about R. L. S., and said that Swinnerton had written a very intelligent book. She had never read one line of Swinnerton except "September" until three days before he came, and then both she and Jane went pell-mell through every novel he had written, one right after another; Jane said that the first ones were really rather dull. Mrs. Ramson told Swinnerton that she read novels in general to find "signposts to guide her in her daily life", and that he was "so rich in signposts."

Myron was very fond of Swinnerton's novel "Nocturne". - "The story was very well handled," he said, "and the end, which might have been so vulgar, was most delicately written" and told Swinnerton so, and the author told Myron, with that restrained emotion the English get across so well, that he had written it by his mother's bedside as she was dying. This gesture quite won Myron and it became one of his favourite literary stories--to prove how the force of the intuition with the real creative artist surpassed all other emotional demands. Swinnerton autographed Myron's copy of "September" a little before he left on the early morning train, sitting in Delia's Oxford chair, and said that Cherry in the book was a real person who was not at all pleased at finding herself there.

Delia's Oxford chair was the highest social test for outsiders. You know what an Oxford chair is, it's made of wicker, deeply cushioned, the seat ten inches high and four feet square. The test was whether you could sit in it gracefully or not. The only way was to recline courageously though it seemed you would never touch the back, and most men looked ridiculous in it sitting just at the very edge, their knees high in the air. Delia filled it very well, and it was after Swinnerton had passed the test with flying colors that Mrs. Ramson said he did not show the lack of a college education.

It was Myron and Jane who brought back the chair from England, and you can imagine what a nuisance it was. They had all kinds of trouble with it at the customs, but finally it reached Otterby no worse for its travels, the wicker in dull gold and the cushions in deep purple, and Delia was very happy in it, for to sit in an Oxford chair had been one of her minor dreams.

An Oxford wicker chair. Delia's was in dull gold and had cushions of deep purple. "The test was whether you could sit in it gracefully or not."

But I was talking about Nadia Schultz Rosenkrantz. She was a musician, a pianist, while her sister was a sculptor in Boston, a great artist, Nadia said. Mrs. Ramson said Mrs. Rosenkrantz understood the "soul of music" and played with "the real dash and sacred fire" that that young lady in the town, Eloise Snow, who had studied abroad and who played Stravinsky and all those other "dissonant, demolishing moderns," simply did not have. Delia had no use for the ultramoderns, "Cézanne's paintings of distorted asses," she said, her fury so great that for once in her life she was vulgar. Myron once started taking the Little Review, but Mrs. Ramson outlawed it out of Otterby as an "indecent, disrespectful periodical." She said that those modern writers like Gertrude Stein

would hang themselves by their own rope; one day they would wake up with a little sense and laugh at themselves to see how ridiculous they had been. "Me and Myself and My Cast-iron Lover," " she would quote contemptuously, "what kind of a woman is that?"

Mrs. Rosenkrantz agreed perfectly with Mrs. Ramson on the ultramoderns; she said Stravinsky, that Bolshevik, would be the "death of music," and her favourite composers were Schubert and Schumann. Especially she liked the songs Schumann wrote the first year of his marriage. "You can tell he had a sensitive artist's soul," she would say; "how he loved and suffered, you can feel it."

Nadia had meant to be a great concert pianist but "love triumphed over art," she said, and she married Mr. Rosenkrantz, who was himself a musician and could understand her artistic temperament.

He was a smallish, gray-haired man who spoke very little, was very kind to his students, and rated in the faculty as a brilliant mathematician. He had written several important pamphlets on higher mathematics, and Mrs. Ramson said he was very sweet and obliging though he did not seem to have "the glowing passion of his people."

The Rosenkrantzes had three children, and the eldest, René, was the Wunderkind. His father had taught him how to play the violin, and the boy played with great facility. He was very proud of himself but a little lazy, and his mother forced him to practice daily and accompanied him at the piano and told him in vivid terms of fame and glory when he became discouraged. But the Rosenkrantzes were getting a little worried about him, as they could teach him no more and Mrs. Rosenkrantz could not separate herself from him by sending him away; still it was obvious that the boy needed a real professor.

Then Jessie Tyler arrived in town, liked it, and settled there, and so saved the day. She had studied with Leopold Auer, was a very fine violinist, and immediately entered the social life with blind, innocent energy. She had lived in cities so long she had forgotten what a small town was like.

XVII

Mrs. Ramson did not find out at first that I played the violin, as my room was in the attic and I practiced with all doors closed when she was out. But after about a month in Otterby she said she heard "vague, lovely sounds like whispers from another world," and both she and Myron thought it was a part of the bewitchment of the house and wanted to believe it that way. But one day I got enthusiastic over a Händel sonata and I let the tone well out of the instrument full and warm. Mrs. Ramson was in the attic at the time searching for a bottle of wine, and she clapped her hands loudly at the end and said "Bravo!" which quite upset me.

"Why, Eric, I didn't know we had a musician in the family! Why, how perfectly lovely! You can play for me and Myron every day! Come down right away and play that. What was it? An overture?-to Myron. He's in his study; he'll be delighted."

She ran down the stairs ahead of me and I followed rather loath to do so. I knew there would be no peace for me from then on. "Oh, Myron, Myron," she cried in a high voice as though the house were on fire, "I've discovered the whispers from the other world!"

Myron emerged from the study slightly bewildered. "What is it, my dear?"

"Eric," she cried, "Eric is a wonderful violinist, and he's been hiding his light under a bushel in the attic, and I just found out, and he can play for us every day, and he is going to play you a beautiful overture now."

Myron saw my face then and he smiled with appreciative surprise at Delia. "But, my dear," he said, "perhaps Eric is like the Japanese flutist."

"Oh, no," said Delia, a little irritated that he did not rise immediately to her high-pitched enthusiasm, "oh, no, I'm sure not."

"What's the Japanese flutist?" I asked. "I don't know that story."

"Oh, it's one of those golden-egg-goose stories," said Delia, anxious for the "overture" to begin.

"Not at all, my dear, not at all," said Myron. "The Japanese flutist," he continued, addressing me, "used to live next door to us when I was living in Japan, and every afternoon he would go to his cherry orchard with his flute and we would listen enchanted - you know that cool, luscious quality of the low tones of the flute. Finally I learned enough Japanese to tell the flutist, whom I met on the road one evening, how much I enjoyed his music. The family scolded me when I told them on arriving home, and sent their apologies, but it was no use. The Japanese flutist never once went to play in the orchard for five weeks after; the shock of learning someone else was listening was too great to be borne."

"Enough of Japanese flutists," said Delia vigorously, "or this overture will be a postlude."

"It is the third sonata of Händel," I said, lifting my bow, "in F major," and forthwith slipped into that gently falling adagio movement.

The hall was an amazing place to play in, because with the stairs it was really two stories high. The acoustics were almost perfect. The tones of the violin expanded beautifully; there was no hollowness and no false echoing. I played not badly and Myron was delighted.

"Music has always seemed more wonderful to me than to other people," said Myron, "for though we have had painters and writers in our family we have never had musicians. The faculty is a more mysterious one to me."

"But, Eric, why didn't you tell us?" said Delia reproachfully. "I should so like to have had you play for James Stephens. An intelligent butler and a real violinist - why, it's perfect," she added. "One of my dreams has always been to have music for my teas in the distance to make a background for the conversation. I am sure that if people subconsciously caught beautiful sounds, their speech would be more beautiful and they would think up more and more beautiful stories to tell. Tell me, Eric, are you free this afternoon?" "Yes, Mrs. Ramson," I said. "Well, then I want you to play for my tea this afternoon," she said. "It will be too delightful, and I'll pay you extra, and I'll make the Greek honey sandwiches with the rosebuds, and I'll call up Mrs. Marsh right now to be sure to come, and we'll have it to be a surprise - oh, Eric! You play here in the hall when you have finished serving, you know, soft little skirls; I'll give you a book of Scotch music and everyone will wonder at the tapestry of lovely sounds behind them." She clapped her hands with the ecstasy of the idea. "Myron, you simply must let me into the study to telephone," she said, walking past him into the room. He turned to me with mock resignation on his features. When Delia Ramson got an idea in her head, there was nothing to do but let her take her course.

XVIII

After the telephoning was over - she must have invited twenty people, which was a highly dangerous proceeding, as Otterby at tea time was always open-house, and on the days when many were invited especially, the same number, uninvited, would arrive also — she went to the kitchen to make sandwiches. This was an almost ceremonial performance: first, the pieces of bread were cut; then, with the aid of a baking-powder can-cover, the pieces of bread were cut into circles, and the parts of bread which remained then were cut into half moons and used as the upper slice, making rather coquettish tomato sandwiches.

With the aid of a baking powder can cover, the pieces of bread were cut into circles.

The Greek honey sandwiches were even more complicated, for they were made of two full circles, save that the upper one had a little round hole in the middle like a doughnut, in which was placed a candied rosebud. The Greek honey was a gift of Mr. Antony Troy Tarpon, a young English instructor, who Mrs. Ramson said was "a gentleman and a real man of the world," and was in a pale green jar of antique lines. Myron said he preferred Mrs. Kivvy's Pure Honey, which came from a local farm. To-day, Mrs. Ramson went even a further step and made caviar sandwiches, which were canapés garnished with slices of pimentoed olives. She always had a qualm in serving caviar or mushrooms because she knew they were really very expensive. She always ordered the caviar and mushrooms in cans by mail from Boston. When students came to dinner or tea - the most promising ones were accorded that privilege by Myron in indulgent moments - Mrs. Ramson got quite interested in one, a sophomore, who, instead of handing in a weekly theme on "Beowulf" handed in a rather nice pen-and-ink drawing of a Viking boat which Myron said "quite caught the quality." Mrs. Ramson said the boy had a "sick soul," and endeavoured to cure him, rousing all kinds of strange, pathological emotions while doing so by inviting him to teas and placing him next to the prettiest professors' daughters - there weren't many - and when this failed, throwing him into conversation with young Mrs. Jayson and the prettier wives of the faculty, but as the boy was stubborn and hung on to his melancholia, which was his only bid for fame in the aesthetic student circle to which he aspired, Mrs. Ramson had no success and at the end of a month or so, even after she had read the dragon story of Cunninghame Graham to him one night all alone in the drawing room and talked about "life" afterwards in the tremolo key, she finally gave him up, "sick soul" and all, as "fundamentally stupid, with a deceptive gloss of intelligence."

But usually when students arrived for dinner she had caviar for the hors d'oeuvre and mushrooms in the soup, and for fear they would not notice she would remind them. "Do you find the Russian caviar appetizing, Mr. Russell?" she would say. Russell was the editor of the daily paper in the college, extremely radical over the necessity of installing the Oxford system of tutors and the suppression of homosexuality in the college. He was tall and heavy, with a tiny head and tiny eyes, and some of his wittier enemies called him "the flaming terrapin." He wore safety pins, quite obviously, at the knees of his linen knickers, and was so serious that Mrs. Ramson said he gave her a headache.

Then, about the mushrooms, she would say to Bob Merlton, who was a millionaire in his own right and went to Fannie Hurst's famous party for Rebecca West just before sailing for Oxford, "Now, Mr. Merlton, those are mushrooms you are eating," but he only thought she was trying to be clever.

Another one of her favourite tricks at a students' party was to balance the silver knives and forks in her hand. "You see how perfectly they are adapted to the hand," she said. "Myron and I searched for years to find the right pattern. You see, the weight is perfectly distributed, so that you cannot suffer the slightest fatigue." These explanations were always followed by a curious silence, for the students never understood that Delia was as impassioned about the slightest detail of her house as she was about entire rooms or the Gothic entrance.

She never served wine to the students, much as would have liked to; "For you cannot," she would say, sipping from her own glass, "really dine without wine. There is no taste left to the meat, for no vegetable offers a sharp enough contrast." She did not serve wine, for in a highly sentimental moment, after two students had been found dead drunk in Mrs. Adams' cellar - they had got in through the window, and the scandal it made in the town was more than a ripple - she called up the president and said that if students should ever come to her house she would not serve them wine but some delicious drink she would think up instead.

XIX

The president did not drink wine, and when he came to the house Mrs. Ramson made the delicious student drink for him. It was an orange pineapple concoction, and she teased him about it at a great summer party she gave in honour of Harold MacDarren, one of the graduates of the college who went off to Oxford and came back with the Redigate prize for a poem on Michelangelo which delighted the professorial heart.

"Do you catch the faint, exquisite echo of Keats in the first ten lines?" said Professor Dundee to me. He was a long, lanky, sour Scotchman opposed to Myron's "conceptual" manner of teaching, whom Mrs. Ramson recognized for his scholastic worth but disliked personally, referring to him always as "that intense red-haired man."

"And then," he continued, "his almost under handed use of the protracted simile, like Matthew Arnold, which gives such a classic spirit to the whole!" Mrs. Ramson, coming up just then, said that all she remembered about Matthew Arnold was that he refused to eat pancakes for breakfast on his trip to America.

Delia remembered that Matthew Arnold had refused to eat pancakes for breakfast on his trip to America.

The young poet himself almost started a mode in the more esoteric coteries of the students and, had he been less cruel in his marks, could have wielded a still greater influence. He was tall and pleasantly consumptive, with dark, curly hair that fell over his forehead romantically; his voice was soft and deep, with an Oxford accent that could be turned off or on, while his Oxford clothes were the delight and despair of all the sartorially interested students.

Until the time for his appearance Mrs. Ramson kept him hidden in the study; he was very nervous anyway about meeting people, and constantly arranged the brown cravat of his blue-and-silver crisscross shirt, and said that he had read his poem so much that it was no longer anything but "patter." Mrs. Ramson said, on hearing this remark, that he was "a really modest poet, rare enough in this day and age."

But he read his poem calmly enough before all the professors, little Professor Kenneth Curman among them tugging his tiny goatee at every Keatsian echo and trying to catch "the philosophic overtones." He was next to the head of the philosophy department and had written a book on "Values," but he had literary pretensions - his theory being that modern literature was the literature of exhaustion - and since he was the neighbour on the other side, Mrs. Ramson invited him to the more elaborate functions of Otterby quite often. He was a pleasant man, fond of gardening, but when he saw the dining room of the Ramsons, with all its painted flowers, he shook his head negatively, saying "Uh, uh, uh-uh," but at the drawing room he merely breathed a long "Ahhh" in complete appreciation of its values.

There was a great deal of applause when MacDarren finished reading his poem, and everybody said he was really very gifted, and he bowed profusely. He looked very well where he was, the green wooden door of the Garden Room for a background, with a single candle in a rose copper socket in the wall to light his pages. The Garden Room itself was a bower of apple blossoms, and Mrs. Ramson surveyed the scene of gentlemen in evening clothes and ladies in décolleté from the first row to the wall in back with real satisfaction.

XX

It may be Mrs. Ramson had it in her head that a tea should follow the classic example of the Mad Hatter, for the big teas at the Ramsons' resembled nothing so much as the childish game of Fruit-Basket-Upset in full progress. One of Mrs. Ramson's entertaining principles was constantly to shift little groups of people so that the bores would be evenly distributed and the clever people not monopolized. It sounded well in principle, but in practice the confusion was unbelievable with more than ten persons in the room, and people whom you carefully avoided would be thrown before you just when you were intensely interested in the conversation of a friend you had not seen for a month.

"The campus," said old Professor Stone, the sole member of the astronomy department, "resembles nothing so much as the stellar system on a highly reduced scale. The various professors are the various planets, and they move in just as definite orbits (due to the college routine) as the heavenly bodies. Some persons you meet once a month at such and such a degree at such and such an hour, others once a week, a few once every six months, and some several times in a day." Professor Stone crossed Mrs. Ramson's orbit about once every two years because accidents would happen. He was a very popular professor because his lectures were filled with dry observations, like "If the tail of a meteor touched the earth it would have the same effect as throwing a feather bed into the ocean."

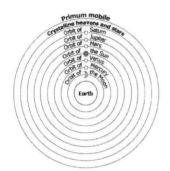

"The various professors are the various planets", said old Professor Stone, "and they move in just as definite orbits."

XXI

The first guest to arrive was little Mrs. Soccy, the Danish woman who painted in water colors and served sweet Scandinavian soups at her dinners. She arrived at four sharp and minced into the drawing room with "Oh, the lovely, lovely flowers! Oh, the lovely lovelies!" I told her Mrs. Ramson would be down directly, knowing very well that Mrs. Ramson would not descend the stairs until four forty-five, if then, for she liked to enter when everyone had arrived, hungry and talking volubly to conceal their impatience. Her entrance was always regal, and I know that, though it was well hidden, she had a deep admiration for Queen Victoria.

I rushed upstairs to tell her, talking through the keyhole, who had arrived. I heard her say, "She's a sweet woman, but isn't it perfectly barbarous, Eric, for a woman to arrive at four for tea? But those Cedar Ridge people..."

I slipped into the drawing room ostensibly to add a log to the fire but really to see what Mrs. Soccy was doing. She was deep in Walter Scott. Myron had put all the classics he never read in the wall-bookcases of the drawing room, where Mrs. Adams said the bindings lent such a decorative note"-and did not even notice me. Mrs. Ramson liked Mrs. Soccy because the latter had made water colours of Otterby outside and in, some of them "quite catching the eighteenth century quality", Myron said. Mrs. Soccy was invited everywhere because she had such an inferiority complex that everyone felt complimented just to be with her. Even the violent Mrs. Beebe always invited her to the musicales, and Mrs. Soccy always turned up in the same dress, her wedding dress of white quilted China silk, and Mrs. Rosenkrantz always complimented her, saying that she was sure Mrs. Soccy was a "real artist," she was so "original."

After four-thirty the guests arrived in droves; there must have been over twenty that day. Mrs. Ramson, up in her room, was exultant and panic-stricken at the same time, for there was nothing she liked more than being the centre of a crowd of chattering people, but she knew the appetites of the starved instructors and she wondered if there would be enough bread.

Feverishly she cut slices of bread and buttered them. It would have to be "simple bread and butter, but so good" for the late guests. Myron had arrived a few moments before she had come down, and he caught the festive spirit about in the house and said he would put on his afternoon clothes, the swallow-tailed coat with the single button, and the wing collar and the black tie, and the gray-striped trousers with pearl-gray spats. "Oh, Myron, what a dear for dressing up!" said Delia, kissing him on the back of his neck. In the kitchen stood all the baskets of sandwiches, ready at last. Some of the baskets were of copper, some of plaited straw, and the layers of sandwiches were larded with white roses and sprigs of myrtle. The three teapots - for Mrs. Ramson served three brands of tea at the big teas: the Jasmine Flower, an emperor's tea, for her dearest friends who knew what real tea was; Orange Pekoe for those who were less favoured or who could not distinguish fine tea from the ordinary, and lastly, in the Delft pot with the cracked cover, was Lipton's for the bores and the people she had invited for policy's sake.

The tea wagon was heavily laden with the Chinese lacquer red cups and saucers, a golden dragon swimming inside them, and all the spoons and the sugar and the little plates of lemon slices symmetrically stuck with tiny cloves for those who liked to take their tea Russian, and a pudgy pitcher of cream for those who preferred the English taste. Mrs. Ramson followed Myron in the matter of tea: in the pure Chinese manner, without anything. "How can you get the pure tea aroma if you taint it with sugar and cream and lemon and spices?" Mrs. Ramson would say, but there were few in the company who heeded.

Finally everything was ready. Marie, the Indian maid, dumb and heavily pretty with her golden skin, had a fresh white lace cap for the occasion, and Mrs. Ramson smiled at her and said she was a "sweet child." She never could have served tea to so many people without getting all the three brands mixed up. I had a hard enough time of it myself. But she was good for serving the second and third classes while I showered attention on the dearest friends and kept a lookout over the general service.

Mrs. Ramson sailed in, but none of the little tables were overturned in the general upset, which was a wonder, for the room was crowded to capacity. "Hello, everyone, and I'm so happy to see you all," said Mrs. Ramson, sitting down in the Oxford wicker chair majestically and almost immediately pressed the push button in the wall which was the servant's bell. This quite obvious gesture put everyone at their ease. I appeared on the scene a moment later and carefully carried the tea wagon down the two steps, the cups rattling in a fearsome manner, and then rolled it across the room to Mrs. Ramson, with an appropriately scornful look on my face for the guests. Marie followed me with a tray of the three pots, and we both stood beside Mrs. Ramson like lieutenants beside a general. As there was such a crowd she refrained from doing what she loved to do, which was to break into the middle of a conversation with "Sugar and cream? Or do you want a Russian lemon?" and instead and just poured the tea, which was served with a tray of sugar and cream and "Russian" lemons.

"Serve Madame Nechicheff first," said Mrs. Ramson; "she is the most elderly lady here and certainly the most gentlewomanly." The Russian lady was the mother of three boys at the college studying in the School of Commerce. The whole family had been ousted by the Bolsheviki She was charming and spoke constantly in French. When her sons met her in the street they always kissed her hand and passers-by would stare. Mrs. Ramson invited her often, though she could not even say "Bon jour", because she liked the idea that Otterby was a refuge for the exiled nobility of Europe.

Then I served Mrs. Marsh, the singer, who Mrs. Ramson said "always had the freshness of a young girl about her." She sang well and had a pleasant contralto voice. She was very gently insistent about the worth of Stravinsky, and played the second piano of the "Sacre" with Eloise Snow. Mrs. Ramson liked her because her husband had made what was for Mrs. Ramson a historic remark: "Otterby does not seem a new house," he said on entering the drawing room for the first time, "for it has been so long in the minds of its creators that it is already old and beautiful." Another remark that Mrs. Ramson cherished was that of Roger Fadden Mote made not long after. There was a silence for a moment in the drawing room while everyone was having after-dinner coffee, and the cuckoo clock which Myron had bought in Switzerland and which hung in the hall sounded loudly and clearly the nine strokes of the hour. "It does not say 'Cuckoo,'" said Roger Fadden Mote. "It says 'Hokku,' which in Japanese means 'everything is beautifully in its place.' "Delia clapped her hands at this, as it was almost too much for the evening, and he had brought them another treasure at the same time: a brass fire-fork from Dartmoor in England with a grinning imp carved atop it.

> The Ramsons' Swiss cuckoo clock did not say "Cuckoo!", it said "Hokku!" in Japanese, stated Roger Fadden Mote.

XXII

Finally all the guests were served, the sandwich baskets demolished, with the roses and myrtle in desolate little heaps, and the second cups began to be poured. Some refused. Young Mr. Edsel, an English instructor who had been to Oxford, never took more than one cup and always refused by saying, with a faultless accent, "Thank you," and you had to guess by the intonation that he had had enough. Then Mr. Candrars, the art instructor who combed his short and thinning hair in straight Theda Bara bangs over his forehead and who always seemed just one degree this side of exhaustion, would say faintly, "No," and sit in farther in the deep armchair, making a slight gesture of negation with his hands. He was a follower of the philosopher Benedetto Croce, in other words, a 'Crocean', and in some strange way had made Botticelli and the Dutch masters attractive and even a matter of common parlance among the more red-blooded men of the college. I heard one of them talking- "This Bottillici, say, he's the kid!" No art criticism was demanded at the final examination, which consisted only in presenting a dozen facsimiles of old masters untitled and you had to give the title, the name of the artist who painted it, his school, and in what museum the picture hung. The head of the art department, Professor Hurd, did not agree with Mr. Candrars at all, but the latter was too popular with the students to be disposed of lightly. Once Myron bought some paintings of a young unknown artist in Washington, two quiet pastoral scenes in the traditional manner, and when Professor and Mrs. Hurd paid an official call, he asked the art professor what he thought of the paintings.

"What's the man's name?" asked Professor Hurd.

"Andrews," answered Myron.

"I've never heard of him," said Professor Hurd. "Is he in any history of art, or are there any monographs about him?"

"Not that I know of," " said Myron. "But what do you think of these paintings? Don't you think they catch a rather pleasant quality?"

"Oh, my dear Professor Ramson," answered Professor Hurd, "you surely can't expect me to pass judgment when I know nothing about the man, now really..."

XXIII

When some of the guests demurred about taking another cup, Mrs. Ramson would call out to me, "Now, Eric, you must use all your seductive powers. I know Mrs. Soccy wants another cup by the way she's saying 'no', but she wants to be tempted." So I said, "You're surely not going to refuse a second cup, are you, Mrs. Soccy?" She giggled nervously, for Mrs. Ramson was watching her so intently. "Why, if you insist..." she answered.

Mrs. Ramson was keeping an eye on Mr. Shorter too, for ever since Mrs. Ramson heard he had read the Bible in class in the manner of Edna St. Vincent Millay (the Bible was part of the freshman course) she was wary about him. He came from Yale and no one knew he was Jewish until his mother came up to visit him. Mrs. Ramson did not like him because he did not have that "courtliness" she had always associated with Yale graduates, and when it became known that he told dirty stories in class his goose was practically cooked. Mrs. Ramson's bête noire was an off-colour story, and one told at the dinner table was enough to chill the atmosphere ten degrees and ruin the evening. I trembled for Professor Jayson when he told that Burne-Jones story about the tattooed lady of the circus. He was a regular green carnation, adored Cocteau, and turned Catholic. His brilliant golf socks were famous where brilliant golf socks were not uncommon. You know the story: Burne-Jones visited the circus and saw this marvelous tattooed woman whose back was a startling reproduction of Da Vinci's "Last Supper." Seven years later the circus returned and he hurriedly went to see the tattooed lady, but, alas, in the seven years' interim she had grown unbelievably fat and all the disciples wore broad smiles on their faces!

Mrs. Ramson turned a horrified face to Myron, but Myron, after a moment's pause, burst into a hearty though disciplined roar of laughter and Professor Jayson beamed on Mrs. Ramson in his triumph, while she merely smiled a little lamely. Myron himself enjoyed Rabelais very much, but in public his most daring joke was a quotation from the Sweet Singer of South Carolina, two lines of a poem entitled "Description of a Maid." "One of the most astounding and precise metaphors I ever heard," said Myron, "were those two lines:

"...........................her leg
Was smooth and hairless as an egg!"[1]

"Myron!" Mrs. Ramson would exclaim reproachfully.

But Mrs. Ramson was more or less powerless before Professor Jayson because, once a professor, he was there to stay and he was a recognized authority on the 1890 period. "What an impossible literature!" Mrs. Ramson would say, thinking of Oscar Wilde.

[1]The Professor evidently didn't know his Herrick. See "Hesperides," No. 350 (published 1648). (*Publisher's Note.*)

XXIV

Everyone was drinking tea comfortably, so Mrs. Ramson clapped her hands to attract attention, which was a Japanese habit which Myron had told her about. She directed her attack on Mr. Shorter. "Now, Mr. Shorter," she said, "charming as she may be, you must not monopolize Mrs. Soccy all afternoon." A ripple of polite laughter ran over the room, as this was a double thrust: Mr. Shorter had not paid the slightest attention to Mrs. Soccy the whole time he was next to her on the great divan (copied from one Delia had discovered in a cottage at Land's End in Cornwall) and, in fact, was engaged a little too arduously in conversation with Mrs. Jayson. "You young Yale men are so intense," she continued. "Now, you change places with Professor Wadman so that you talk to Madame Nechicheff. Don't say you don't speak French," she added gaily, as a little sweet after sour, "for everyone tells me you speak it beautifully."

Professor Wadman, who was a habitué of Otterby at tea time, reluctantly ceased his suave flow of French, which he loved to speak, and did as Mrs. Ramson bade, sitting down beside Mrs. Soccy resignedly to talk about Constantinople. He had lived there for ten years, a portly gentleman who was fond of the word "cacaphony" and who was as English as a mutton chop. His greatest social achievement was the reading out loud of Bernard Shaw, for his imitation of the cockney accent was perfect, and Mrs. Ramson cried for joy at his rendition of the flower girl, saying he was really a profound student of the drama. "No man," she said, "can be truly called a master of his craft unless he is able to play with it. I think that is an 'infalayable' rule."

"A what?" asked Mrs. MacWhoog, the wife of the head of the music department.

"How is it that musicians never know their Barrie?" replied Mrs. Ramson with polite reproof. "It's the policeman in 'A Kiss for Cinderella,' who makes the rule for finding out if a lady is a gentlewoman or not. If she puts her handkerchief down her bosom she is, but if the handkerchief goes in the pocket there's no hope. The rule is 'infalayable.'"

"Oh, how charming!" said Mrs. MacWhoog, and she laughed. She had a laugh like her name, hollow and deep and throaty, and Mrs. Ramson shuddered to hear it. She said later it disturbed the rhythm of the drawing room to such an extent that it did not seem the same for half an hour after.

Myron entered just then, impeccable, and as he was the only man there in afternoon clothes, even a little exotic. He immediately sat down by Mrs. Adams, a sallow Southern woman who always wore long black gowns and very chic black hats, and smoked long Russian cigarettes. She was smoking one then, and the smoke floating in two thin streams from her long, delicate nose gave her an obvious superiority over the other more virtuous ladies in the room. Mrs. Ramson tried time and again to smoke, but she always puffed the cigarette with pitiful despairing gasps and spat the smoke out as soon as she had it in her mouth. She seldom refused a cigarette when it was offered her, however, and would sit posing with it awhile and then would roll it all to pieces, saying that she reserved cigarettes for "tragic occasions like funerals."

Mrs. Ramson's friendship for Mrs. Adams was almost purely political, because Mrs. Adams, due to her knowledge of Early American furniture, was called all over the United States to verify certain pieces and to buy for collectors and made so much money she was forever dashing off to France and England, where she made again as much by writing travel books for antique lovers. Then, too, Mrs. Adams had a lot to do with the furnishing of Otterby because she knew so much about dealers that she was able to put her hand on just what Delia wanted. But Mrs. Ramson said that to be with Mrs. Adams in New York it was just "taxi after taxi." She said, too, that while not denying Mrs. Adams was very clever, her daughter, Jane Ramson, really had the better "feel" for antiquities, although, of course, she did not have the erudition. But then Jane was only eighteen.

Myron was very fond of Mrs. Adams because she played so admirably into his hand when he essayed the witty gentleman. They were talking gaily about New York, which city Myron liked more than any other in the world, always having a few secret regrets that Delia preferred the country life. Two or three times in the winter, when life in the town became too dull, he would suddenly announce that he was leaving for New York on the next train, and Delia always wrote him a letter telling him how Scarot had barked himself into a fury over his departure. Scarot could get very temperamental and froth at the mouth, for he always thought that when Myron left with his suitcase he was going to Europe. And why had he forgotten his rubbers when he knew how delicate his throat was? And could he get some bars of that special Parisian soap which was so good? She had forgotten the name but he would remember, the one with the green wrapper, and how lonely she was without him.

Myron always departed wearing a handsome mauve-gray overcoat and one of his London tweeds and the wide-brimmed light gray fedora. He had bought his suitcase in Paris, one of those huge pigskin affairs, a young trunk, and it was belabelled with every colour from hotels of every land.

He returned tired but up to the minute on all the literary happenings, having seen the newest plays: "That man O'Neill likes to see raw flesh in suffering" and heard talk about the newest books and the newest restaurants, and would talk glowingly in class about New York for three days after.

The Professor would suddenly announce that he was going to New York on the next train.

XXV

Mrs. Ramson got up from the Oxford chair and went to the alcove, where Professor Marsh was sitting with Mrs. Moorhead. "And what have you psychologists been discovering today?" she questioned brightly, drawing up a bench, the one that was upholstered in a Roman pattern costing ten dollars a yard, yellow and gold and purple stripes; Mrs. Ramson said it had "all the old galley feeling".-While Mrs. Moorhead excused herself and said she had to see Mrs. Jayson that minute or she would forget the errand her husband, who had not been able to come, had sent her on. She knew perfectly well that Mrs. Ramson had changed places to show Myron that she was not alone in the world, but Myron kept right on talking about his garden to Mrs. Adams.

Mrs. Ramson could contain herself no longer and, abruptly turning from Professor Marsh, who was in the midst of his favourite literary theory, that "Babbitt" was not the result of the author but of the self-consciousness of the Middle-West, Delia said he was a brilliant man, Marsh, but that he had great "gaps" in his literary equipment.She said very audibly to Myron: "What were you saying to Mrs. Adams about our garden?"

"I was saying," said Myron, annoyed at the interruption but retaining, as always, his good humour and perfect politeness, "how pleasant it would be if we could add a little Cupid in pink marble instead of the granite bird bath at the centre of the Saint George Cross."

"Myron!" exclaimed Mrs. Ramson, vanquished and still admiring his apt answer; "and you accuse me of being Victorian!"

The Saint George Cross was the flagged stone walk in the sunken garden on the south side of the house. Myron was sure for a long time that it was not pointing correctly, but finally, after much reference work in the library, which was an old cobblestone building with several turrets which made fine hiding places for books, it was found that the cross was placed correctly, and Myron took his Sunday morning walks in the garden with his cane and light flannels (another Brazilian heritage) with greater pleasure than before.

Mrs. Ramson did not stay very long with Professor Marsh but moved over to Mr. Shorter, who was talking to Eloise Snow, and, judging from the way Miss Snow was saying, "Oh, really, Mr. Shorter!" and laughing, Mrs. Ramson thought it was high time to intervene. In crossing over to the divan, she cast a brilliant smile on Madame Nechicheff, who kept saying, "Oui, oui," with polite wonderment at Mrs. Soccy, who heroically persisted in asking her what time it was in Russian.

Eloise Snow was very pretty as long as she did not have a cold, which was, alas, quite often. Professor Wadman was boasting that moment how he had not suffered from one because he had taken "cold preventer," a new hypodermic, very expensive, but after one had lived in Constantinople so long the highest precautions were not too dear, and after all what was more valuable than good health? And she was that English type of beauty, piles of auburn hair, a long, narrow face, large blue eyes, and bright red lips Oh, Mr. Shorter was having a good time, and crossed his legs carefully (he was in baggy-kneed knickerbocker trouses, another thing Mrs. Ramson abhorred in the drawing room) to show that he wore Scotch garters with woolen tassels at his knee. Eloise Snow was a Smith College girl, to begin with, which Mrs. Ramson considered an almost impossible handicap. "The girls that come out of that place," she would say, "have such a stiff posture and seem so gauche in matters feminine." But as Eloise Snow was one of the few marriageable girls in the town, she could not help taking a certain interest.

Eloise wrote poetry as well as playing the "demolishing moderns," and she would read specimens on the slightest provocation. She read, very breathlessly:
"And I,
A candle
Searching for a moth "

"Why, Eloise," said Mrs. Ramson, casting another dazzling glance on Mr. Shorter, which that young man returned with equanimity ... he had money (that was the trouble) and could not learn the proper attitude ... "how can you leave a handsome poet like Harold MacDarren all alone moping in the corner?"

Harold raised his head at hearing his name; he had been enjoying his detachment, and when he saw Eloise he smiled without enthusiasm, as it seemed every hostess in town was trying to make a match, but he had been to Oxford too long ever to want to marry.

Eloise quitted Mr. Shorter then and sat down by Harold with an avid smile. "Do you think 'The Wasteland' is a great poem?" she began ambitiously, and Mrs. Ramson drew in her shoulders at this terrific beginning. "Oh, children," she called over to them, as it gave her a pleasant maternal feeling to address all under thirty this way: "don't plunge into such a melancholy subject. That man Eliot is only a vers de société man, and not a very clever one at that."

Myron raised his eyebrows at this. He drew the line at "Sweeney among the Nightingales" but he admitted "The Wasteland" had disturbed him. Still, he was loath to quit Mrs. Adams, so he held his peace and went on talking about his youth on the pampas.

"Do you think The Wasteland is a great poem?" she began ambitiously.

As the tea drinking seemed definitely over, Mrs. Soccy was making the signs preliminary to departure, such as looking all over for a clock. Madame Nechicheff at last did not have a wrist watch. Mrs. Ramson ignored her gestures as ill-bred; "but then these Swedish women are different," she would say (the Danes, Swedes, and Norwegians were all one to her); and then she gave me the high sign to begin "the tapestry of lovely sounds" in the hall. So I left the drawing room and went upstairs for the violin.

I did not play any Scotch "skirls" that day, as Mrs. Ramson had forgotten to give me the book, and I never really caught on to the strathspeys in the right way- "You have to be borne with it," Mrs. Ramson would say, thumping out the tune with one finger on the sick, rickety piano in the Garden Room. So I began with a Haydn minuet, but it did not have the effect that Mrs. Ramson wanted. Everyone was so surprised at the music that conversation ceased abruptly, and even Mrs. Ramson, who talked on valiantly for the first half of the piece, was forced to stop, for everyone must have been staring at her.

When the minuet was over, someone started a feeble, tentative applause (for no one knew quite what to do under the circumstances), which must have been quickly squelched by a look from Mrs. Ramson, who further added: "It's just Eric playing; only I'm sure he'll stop if you listen. You're just supposed to be listening subconsciously so that the music will suggest beautiful thoughts to you."

This new wrinkle of Delia's having been satisfactorily explained to the guests, they took the cue and began talking again. As I prepared my music for the next number, I heard Delia continue: "You know, Eric is a little like the Japanese flutist, only instead of a cherry orchard he was playing in the attic, and I only discovered him this morning and was afraid he would never play again. Oh, you don't know the story about the Japanese flutist? It was when Myron was in Japan ..."

I plunged into a violent Hungarian dance.

XXVI

In the midst of one of my pieces the doorbell rang, and I heard Mrs. Ramson scramble across the drawing room to ring the servants' bell so that Marie would open the door. I kept on playing then. Mrs. Ramson said later she was glad I had done so, for to have broken the "flow" of the room that moment would have been a pity.

It was Mrs. Rosenkrantz, with another younger women whom I had not seen before, and I kept on playing. Mrs. Rosenkrantz had begun making copious apologies to Marie even before she was in the room, galoshes and all, and then stopped short at seeing me and hearing the music. She looked at me over the music rack with smothering sweetness as though my violin had been her discovery, not Mrs. Ramson's, and as she stepped into the drawing room I heard her say, "Oh, I can't say a word. I'm overcome, Mrs. Ramson. You're so original! Music, and such a music, in the hall even!" and then, confusedly, "Oh, I forgot, may I present" - I played pianissimo to hear the name - "Miss Jessie Tyler?"

"So sorry you didn't come before, my dear," said Mrs. Ramson. "There's only bread and butter left for you. It's very simple, but just the same so good."

I stopped playing the violin immediately, for I knew this Miss Tyler had studied with Leopold Auer for years and I did not want to be playing then until I knew her better and could explain my position. Mrs. Ramson had told me she didn't want any "overtures" for the tea, just light music, old fashioned dances, and tender folk songs. "Träumerei" was just the thing, she said; Schumann was one of her favourite composers anyway.

Eric knew that Jessie Tyler had been a pupil of the famous violinist Leopold Auer, so he needed to explain his position.

XXVII

"Scarot!" called Mrs. Ramson threateningly; "come here this instant, naughty Scarot!"

The tea guests smiled sympathetically.

"You mustn't be bothered, Mr. MacDarren," said Delia sweetly. "Professor Scraggs of the biology department explained to me that there is nothing wrong with Scarot; he was just experiencing a 'muscular reaction'."

Every night Scarot slept in the same bed (at the foot) with Delia and Myron. That is, every night except about once every two weeks, and those nights Scarot would be very much excited, whining and squealing like no animal of this earth, and it took all kinds of special enticements to get him into the study, where, once locked in, he kept up a furore for a long while and would be very grouchy all the next day.

Once Delia, a sudden caprice seizing her, locked Scarot in the study without turning on the light either in there or in the hall. Myron had already gone up to bed. And then Delia went upstairs. Myron came rushing down, half dressed, a few moments later, and hurriedly entered the study, but it was too late, as the damage was done. Scarot made a triumphant exit bearing three mangled examination papers in his mouth, and the study looked as though a hurricane had struck it.

Myron always marked the examinations in the study and, as he would have fifty or sixty at a time, put them in neat piles on the floor all around him, the A's, the B's, the B-minuses; but as that night he had not finished and was very tired, he had not troubled to pick up those he had marked, and Scarot had wreaked a terrible vengeance on them. After that episode Scarot was housed in the Garden Room, where he could damage only the wicker chairs.

XXVIII

All the guests except Mrs. Rosenkrantz and Miss Tyler had left, as it was after seven o'clock, so Mrs. Ramson called me in. At such moments I was no longer the butler but was introduced as "the young man of the family," and while Mrs. Rosenkrantz and Miss Tyler looked at me and talked, she smiled with affectionate pride.

"Miss Tyler says she only got a whiff of your violin and she is curious to see it. Why didn't you continue playing?"

"It was a case of the Japanese flutist," I replied.

"Oh, Eric," said Mrs. Ramson, highly pleased with this answer, "you mustn't let a mere story influence you so."

I excused myself then to get my violin while she told them the story. This Miss Tyler, in the few moments I had seen her and been introduced to her, impressed me as a delightful person. She was not pretty but she had a nicely shaped head with short bobbed hair of pleasant lustre in the candlelight. She was dressed with excessive neatness in dark blue (at least, that was the impression), she was not very tall, and her voice was low and restrained, with a soft Canadian accent.

She took the violin from my hands very gracefully and tenderly, which is a rare thing to see, as a violin is more awkward to take hold of than a baby. "The A string's got a lovely tone," she said, and admired the beautiful golden grain in the wood of the back.

Then she took the bow and played that gay little minuet of Pugnani. She played very neatly, very precisely, with a clear, bright tone that was not lacking in warmth.

Mrs. Ramson clapped her hands. "Oh, it's too wonderful, two violinists in one day! How long are you going to be in town, Miss Tyler?"

"Oh, indefinitely," she answered. "The life seems pleasant here and I'm tired of the cities."

"Well, can you come to tea with your violin Friday week?" said Mrs. Ramson. "We'll have a real musicale in the Garden Room. Mrs. Rosenkrantz can accompany you and play some of her beautiful Schumann too; and, my dear, you'll wear your Russian costume, won't you, to give a note of color to the room?" she finished up, turning to Mrs. Rosenkrantz.

The latter agreed enthusiastically. She foresaw that Miss Tyler would be a real social triumph for her, and Miss Tyler acquiesced also, saying she would be glad to meet the people of the town, she was sure they would be charming.

She turned to me a little before leaving: "And won't you come to see me? I am at Mrs. Borsch's house, that new one near the old Catholic church". At that moment the old Catholic church was being converted into a Jewish fraternity house. "We can play some duets together. Do you like the Bach Concerto for two violins?"

I finally agreed to go on condition that I be considered a pupil. Mrs. Rosenkrantz smiled at me in a new way and rather mysteriously.

XXIX

Jane was the daughter and she had her father's will. When she was little she suffered from heart trouble, but now, as Delia said, "due to our careful supervision, she is quite robust." She never went to school. Myron was quite strong on this point; I remember one Sunday morning, after a faculty meeting had not gone off the way he had hoped, he was very nettled and said emphatically, "Sometimes I think a college education is no education at all, but rather a step in the wrong direction!" No, Jane had the "best of two continents," as Mrs. Ramson phrased it. She had travels in Europe and for her teachers "the greatest men in the world," Myron Ramson and Roger Fadden Mote. The latter taught her French, which Jane spoke beautifully, and he also laid the foundation of a love for Paris that culminated later and which Mrs. Ramson found so disturbing.

"The young generation is not the same," she explained to Mrs. Johnsen and Mrs. Whitlock, who were come to a private tea where the scandal of the town was once more rehearsed. Mrs. Whitlock lived in the Faculty Apartments, and her window gave over the court to Mrs. Furze's. "Only last Sunday," she said, "not only Mrs. Furze and Mr. Furze", who was known on the campus as "Smut" Furze, for his classes were the raciest of all, "but young Mr. Marin as well, were promenading in the apartment absolutely naked, and I went over to borrow a cup of sugar, and then there was a flurry of excitement!"

"It's a pity that Mr. Marin should get in such a circle," said Mrs. Ramson. Mr. Marin was the instructor in the dramatic department, which was a very difficult job, for the boys who took the feminine rôles in the plays were so jealous of one another that he was constantly embroiled in various intrigues, and he was one of Mrs. Ramson's blasted hopes. He was a stout young man and looked like Louis Quatorze in shell-rimmed glasses, and he could talk for hours about his theatrical experience without stopping. Mrs. Ramson had tried to make a match for him with Eloise Snow, never dreaming in the world that he was a divorced man, and Marin got in very deep with Eloise, staying at the Snows' until two and three in the morning. Mrs. Ramson even gave a tea for them specially, and Eloise wore such a triumphant red velvet dress that everyone was sure the engagement would be announced. And then someone found out that Mr. Marin had been married before, and Eloise retired from public view for a month, while Marin went on a hurried trip to New York as his father was very ill.

"No, the young generation is certainly different," repeated Delia. "There's my daughter now, a real gentlewoman; yet, rather than have a home and a maid, I so wanted the last for her, for the 'bloom' wears off so quickly after marriage, she prefers to save her money and go off to Paris for the summer."

"Really!" said Mrs. Johnsen, whose husband was in Paris that very moment, a white-haired history professor who stuttered and hyphenated all his words audibly with an "ah...". I counted a hundred of them in one hour, making little marks on a paper while he was talking on what he called "the red peril" to Myron. He was in Paris as an expert at the tail end of the Peace Commission, and when he came back he gave several talks on "The Perils of Paris" for the Y. M. C. A. Sunday Evening Get-togethers, and denounced the city as a most unchristian place and the last place to visit for any ambitious, clean-minded young man.

One of the young men there at one of these meetings, however, did not heed his advice but went to the French capital for a year and lived with a little French girl named Madeleine. He wondered even if he should marry her, but decided not to one day when she expressed surprise at the name of his university.

"You come from there?" she asked.

"Yes," he answered. "Why, do you know any of the boys?"

"No," she said, "but an old professor with white hair who stuttered and said 'ah' always, oh, he was nice-for several months he was here."

The wickedness which brooded over Paris, 'a most unchristian place', was discussed and warned against, but Jane was determined to go there for the summer regardless.

XXX

It was when Myron went to the Bahamas that Clarence Rollinson arrived, for though he was a young man he was the only one, it seemed, qualified to carry on Myron's work in modern literature. As lodgings in the town were difficult to procure then, in mid-semester, he stayed at the Ramson's house. He did not stay at Otterby, for this is ancient history I am telling. Jane was only a little girl then of fourteen or so.

Mrs. Ramson speedily initiated Mr. Rollinson into the household: how she made roses of butter for the table in the French way, only she didn't do it for the French reason, to pretend there was a lot when there was only a little, but because it made the butter more palatable, and how she always had a clean hearth to keep up an old English tradition, and how she cut up the lettuce always in little pieces so that the guests would not be embarrassed. Young Mr. Rollinson was very pliable and did errands for Delia and got strawberries out of season as a reward and wrote a poem about Scarot which definitely placed him at that moment as "the young man of the family."

He was not a handsome man, but his conversation was sensitive and amusing, and he spent his summers with the Ramsons in the Blue Ridge Mountains of Virginia, which was Delia's native state, in their little summer cabin. For one summer there Delia was impassioned over photography. "It is an art that has all the elements of painting except colour, and yet the technique is so much more simple," she said. Delia had experimented in water colours when she was younger, but not very successfully. Myron sketched fairly well and had many notebooks full of drawings of old English houses he had made when he went bicycling through that country with Clarence Rollinson which were part of the long preparation for Otterby. But the photographic craze did not last long, and the camera was sent up to the attic. Delia made enough pictures for a big volume, mostly of Myron awake and sleeping and staring with arms akimbo over the Blue Ridge Mountains, and that was all. Jane went around barefooted in those days, and copied the English classic poems in a notebook while Delia instructed her in "matters feminine."

But when Delia discovered that Jane was falling in love with Clarence, that was another story. Jane was sent off to Europe with her father for a year in order to forget she had ever known Clarence Rollinson, and the latter took up lodgings in another part of the town. But Clarence kept on writing letters, and the farther Jane travelled away from him, the more she was in love.

Jane fell in love with Clarence Rollinson when she was only fourteen, and Professor Ramson had to take her to Europe for a year to get over it. She never attended school.

XXXI

I got to know Jessie Tyler very well. We played violin together often and I taught her to ski. That was a nice bright winter morning; the air was sharp, and the snow just right, not too sticky and not too slippery. We went up to Copely Hill, about five miles away, a steady climb going up and a thrilling descent round and round the hill coming back. Jessie caught on to skiing quickly, and liked it. When I had an extra hour in the evening, I usually went over to her room at Mrs. Borsch's to play or talk or read, for she had a fine little library.

"Where are you going with your violin, Eric?" Mrs. Ramson would call out the kitchen window, since when it was cold weather, she liked the radiator seats of the breakfast nook.

"To Jessie's," I replied a little shortly, for I did not like to be called back once I had left the house.

"Eric, come here," said Mrs. Ramson then, a little solemnly. "Where are you going?" she asked again, standing now in the cold hall of the kitchen, which served as a kind of butler's pantry.

"To Jessie's," I replied.

"No, Eric," she said, "to Miss Tyler's. If she is your friend, you must have respect enough to talk of her in public properly."

"But she has given me permission to use her first name," I said defensively, having already sensed the reason for her displeasure. "The modern girls don't stick so to formalities."

"That's where they make a mistake," answered Delia, "and it's up to the fine gentlemen of the land to set them right again. Miss Tyler is a charming girl and I am happy you have made such a pleasant friendship, but you know she has mixed up so long with 'modern' people in the cities, in that dreadful place called Greenwich Village, that she has a little forgotten the manners of the fine people which her family represents". (Her father was president of some Canadian university.)"And I wish, Eric, you would just delicately hint, very delicately, like a gentleman, that it is getting increasingly difficult for me to receive her, for even Mrs. Heron, you know, last week did not invite her to the luncheon she gave for the girls of the town, as some of the girls said they could not come if Miss Tyler was there."

The President's wife. Mrs. Hopkins ("Mrs. Heron" in the novel) did not invite Jessie to luncheon because some of the girls of the town said they would not come if Miss Tyler was there.

"How absurd!" I said, rather angrily. "There's not a girl in town that can come up to her, and you know they're just jealous of her success here."

"Eric!" said Mrs. Ramson, and her eyes lit up with a warning glow of anger.

I saw I had been too vehement, so I cut my voice down and continued, very coldly and recklessly: "As to the social life of the town, Miss Tyler has already seen what a sham it is and has no interest in it. She is an artist and above the petty gossip of the place. And I am sure, too, that the real people will not stop inviting her even if she does seem a little eccentric."

Mrs. Ramson was, of course, furious. "I am very disappointed in you, Eric," she said. "I thought you would be a gentleman enough to see that I have only the best intentions for Miss Tyler. There is already too much talk going around the town about you and her, and I merely wanted to save you some unpleasantness."

And she turned and closed the kitchen door with a slam.

Anything might happen to a young person in "that dreadful place called Greenwich Village."

XXXII

Jessie was glad to see me but she was not very happy, and I found out then, by some questioning, that she had been snubbed that day at a tea by old Mrs. Finckner and Mrs. Johnsen, two of a kind. I, of course, did not tell her what Mrs. Ramson had said, for I saw she was more annoyed with herself for being annoyed than anything else. But in a small town ordinary social relationships become so magnified in importance that they are distorted and it is difficult to find the right perspective.

Jessie had entered the town quietly as an acquaintance of Mrs. Rosenkrantz, and the formal musicale that Mrs. Ramson had given for her gave her a strong start in the life of the upper circles of the community. She was invited to Mrs. Heron's, the president's wife, right away, and to the Hollanshores' and the Snows' and the Marshes' very soon after. Oh, but Mrs. Ramson praised that musicale! The Garden Room was completely filled with the teaching staff of the English department, even to the detested "Smut" Furze, besides Professor Curman from next door and the other neighbours, Professor and Mrs. Beebe and Chaplain Jellie and Mrs. Heron. Mrs. Ramson had the Garden Room carefully arranged in rows of chairs, and she saw to it that "Smut" Furze had one of the most uncomfortable ones while Mrs. Heron was installed in a green wicker armchair, in equal rank with Mrs. Ramson, in the first row.

Since the affair was held in the Garden Room and as it was a musicale, which was a rare thing in Otterby, Mrs. Ramson felt she had to wear something special, and as her new dresses had not yet arrived because her dressmaker was an impoverished Virginia lady of high degree living in the Blue Ridge Mountains, "just as good as a Paris modiste," and one of her best examples of economy when she was giving instructions on married life to the brides on Saturday flower-arranging mornings, she wore her black velvet dress with black lace sleeves and a black velvet-and-lace cap like the old doges of Venice. She wore the cap like a crown, and came down at the last minute breathless, as usual; but the chairs were so packed in the Garden Room that the men could not get up easily, and she said gaily, waving her hand to Mrs. Marsh in the back, "Hello, everyone; don't bother to get up."

And then, beaming all over the room, she sat down heavily and said to Mrs. Rosenkrantz, who was self-consciously waiting on the piano stool in her highly embroidered linen costume with the wooden beads, "You may begin, my dear. Is it the Schumann?" (Jessie was to play second and was waiting upstairs in the study. Scarot had been locked up in Delia's bedroom for fear that he would "sing" too much.)

"I adore Schumann," said Mrs. Ramson in an audible whisper to Mrs. Heron at her side, when the first number was half finished. Mrs. Heron nodded with an affirmative smile. Mrs. Rosenkrantz, who was playing one of the songs Schumann had written in the first year of his married life, started out firmly enough on the rickety piano that the tuner had done his best with, but at the sound of Mrs. Ramson's voice so close to her she got rattled, hesitated for a breathless second, recaptured a melody, but a wrong one, so accelerated the tempo immediately to hide her error, made a few arpeggios in an enharmonic key, then went through an amazing and most un-Schumannlike modulation with some wild Zingara chords, once more caught the theme, and finished solemnly and sentimentally on a key far distant from the original.

"Marvellous, my dear!" said Mrs. Ramson, rising impulsively and kissing her.

"Such a touch!" breathed Mrs. Jayson to Mrs. Marsh, who smiled a little wryly, as her husband was a much better pianist and she knew how Mrs. Rosenkrantz had really played.

Mrs. Heron said nothing but smiled very sweetly and blankly at Mrs. Rosenkrantz, who perhaps, despite all her efforts, would never enter the presidential home. Then Mrs. Rosenkrantz's hope came down the stairs, namely Jessie.

Jessie was pretty that day, dressed in a bright pink frock with a stiff, wide silken skirt, and she was in agreeable possession of herself before the mass of faces.

She raised her bow with that abrupt but graceful manner of the wrist and began the Pugnani "Praeludium and Allegro," with its vital and surprising intervals. Talk stopped. Then swiftly the tempo changed into the short staccato runs of the Allegro, and Mrs. Ramson began to tap her fingers to the time. The Allegro mounted, and then suddenly flowered into vibrant chords. Mrs. Ramson rolled in her chair with ecstasy, and kept turning around and beaming on various people as if to say, "There, now, isn't she a wonder?"

The applause was long and sincere. Jessie had won success in a single bound.

"The way her bow grips the strings!" said Mrs. Jayson to Mrs. Marsh. "Did you notice that?"

Just then, above all the clapping hands and nodding heads, Mrs. Marsh caught the eye of Jessie, made the gesture of shaking hands, and called out, "Bravo!" The room was all animation. Even "Smut" Furze, usually of morose features, had turned to Mr. Shorter with a smile on his face, saying, "Say, she's the real stuff!"

But above all the racket rose Mrs. Ramson's serene high judgment: "My dear, you are the most wonderful violinist I have ever heard! Yes, the most marvellous! But I must hear that overture again! You must, you must play it again for me, and I beg you, I command you, this minute!" When Mrs. Ramson employed that tone, there was nothing to do but yield, and Mrs. Rosenkrantz, who was smiling relievedly that the difficult accompaniment had gone off so well, paled at the thought of going through the piece all over again. Jessie acquiesced, however, with a boyish bob of her head to the hostess, and once more the Garden Room was flooded over with the tones of the violin under her sounding bow.

XXXIII

As I was saying, after the musicale Jessie was a success. The Arts Club immediately invited her to give a recital in the Little Theatre, which she did a few weeks after. I was not able to go, but the recital was a success, too. She did not play with Mrs. Rosenkrantz then, but with Morris Hampden.

Few people suggest the professions they are engaged in, but of all who looked unlike a musician I think Morris Hampden was the one. His enemies always referred to him as "the misguided prizefighter." He was square-headed, Scotch, with scratchy red hair and a burr in his mouth, a tiny snub nose, and piercingly blue eyes which seemed lost in his face; and he constantly smoked cigarettes through his nose, which gave a terrifying dragon expression, and the women in the Community Orchestra which he conducted trembled before him.

Yet, beneath the shell of terror in which he had incased himself was a singularly gentle and sensitive man. Mrs. Ramson even awed him, and he was like a lamb in the drawing room. "There's not a gentleman of my acquaintance," said Mrs. Ramson whenever the subject of music was discussed, "who serves sandwiches so unobtrusively as Mr. Hampden. Just when you think a lady is in need, you find she has just been served." This is what happened at occasional teas

I did not serve. As they were held every day: "What an absurd idea those Cedar Ridge people have," Delia would say with amused contempt, "to serve tea only on Sunday afternoons! I don't know what I'd do without my tea. It can save any day from being completely ruined, and it gives you just that relaxation necessary to be brilliant in the evening!" I missed some of them, having other work to do at times, and for a long while Marie, the Indian maid, was not very well.

'There's not a gentleman of my acquaintance who serves sandwiches so unobtrusively as Mr. Hampden,' according to Delia. The real Maurice Hampden of the novel was Professor Maurice Frederic Longhurst, born at Windsor in England in 1887, came to Dartmouth in 1921 as Director of Music and of the Community Chorus (later the Handel Society), and promoted to full Professor of Music in 1924. He retired in 1954 and died in 1960. He was one of the people in Dartmouth whom Bravig Imbs most admired. *Photo courtesy of David T. Robinson of the Dartmouth Handel Sociey, with grateful thanks.*

Clarence Rollinson, who did not like music very much, said it was worth going to the annual oratories just to watch the high collar of Mr. Hampden, who conducted, slowly wilt, crumple, and disappear.

Hampden was a man of great energy, and it was President Heron who discovered him while visiting the Vanderbilts at their Alabama home. Hampden was their organist, and Heron brought him back to town with him when he returned, making a complete upset in the music department, which had been quietly going along doing nothing for some years. With the advent of Hampden, the head of the music department, MacWhoog, began a terrific feud with him out of pure jealousy, and the town took sides.

Mr. MacWhoog was a very imposing man with a deep voice and a Teddy Rooseveltian manner, and he was president of the town's Rotary Club (made up mostly of grocers and haberdashers). His favourite gesture was to reserve the best seat in the college assembly hall for himself at the big concerts like the Vladimir de Pachmann one, and then, just at the last minute, stride handsomely to his place.

Professor MacWhoog (real name Professor Leonard Beecher McWhood) was a very imposing man with a deep voice and a Teddy Rooseveltian manner. Here is a photo of him in 1922, the year Bravig Imbs arrived.

He was strong for advertising also, and his poster for the De Pachmann concert was pointed out as a model of convincingness to the students in the Business School. It was a bright red poster with black printing:

Who is the greatest pianist in the world?
DE PACHMANN.

Who is the greatest interpreter of Chopin in the world?
DE PACHMANN.

Who is now on his last farewell tour in America?
DE PACHMANN.

Will he play in our Assembly Hall? YES!

Will he play a program of Chopin exclusively? YES!

Will his appearance here be absolutely his last appearance in America? YES!

ARE WE GOING! I'LL SAY WE ARE!

Certainly the De Pachmann concert was the most chic concert of the year, and there were fifty people in line early in the morning at the bookstore the first day the tickets were sold, and soon there were none left. One of the rich boys there decided to outwit MacWhoog and bought twenty-five tickets for the first rows and then invited twenty-four of his friends to a dinner (to be followed by the concert) at one of the new tea rooms of the town. The dinner was not at "The Plaid Cow," which was getting a little old-fashioned, but the newest one, "At Ye Olde Green Lanthorne." "The Plaid Cow" started on a rainy day, and three graduates of Smith College ran it. It was a great success for a while, for the girls were pretty and the peach jam with nuts was really good. Mrs. Ramson said she thought they might have found "a more alluring name," and as the girls were Smith girls she did not take much stock in the venture. "The Three Plaid Cows," as the girls were called, had a big success at the fraternity dances, however, but after six months or so their novelty wore off, except for a few faithful tea topers, and new tea houses began to spring up in all parts of the town.

Murphy's on the Green at 11 South Main Street in Hanover is a present day restaurant believed to be situated in the premises of one of the tea and dining rooms mentioned by the author.

But, talking about fraternity dances, I remember the first one I ever attended. I dressed in my Tuxedo and, as usual, went to search for Delia to tie my bow. She was not in the drawing room, and Professor Ramson, in the study, said that Mrs. Ramson had felt chilly and had gone to bed but that she surely was not asleep and, if he remembered rightly, had expressed a special desire to see me before I left. So I went upstairs to the green door of the bedroom, and Scarot gave an answering yawp to my knock.

"Is that you, Myron?" questioned Mrs. Ramson.

"No, it is Eric," I answered.

"Oh, do come in. I'm just resting."

The room was softly lit with the single rose lamp at Mrs. Ramson's bedside, and several new novels were spread on the yellow counterpane. She tied my tie and I could see that the soft effulgence of the light was repeated in her mood. She spoke very tenderly: "Now Eric, you are going to your first fraternity dance, and both Myron and I are so happy you found a society of young men to your liking, but you know this first dance is in the nature of a test, and I know you'll come out with flying colours, but all your 'brothers' will know after tonight whether you are a real gentleman or not. I know you are, but you mustn't slip on this first occasion, for that would be so disastrous for your college career. You're going to be tempted tonight, oh, I know, tempted to do things which no gentleman would ever think of doing, and I don't just mean the punch bowl either. You certainly have to be careful of the girls you meet today, and you know no college man invites the girl he intends to marry to these dances. It is always the second-best, and sometimes these Smith girls, you know, do not come from our best homes and have, how shall I say?, imbibed some strange modern ideas and they do not conduct themselves in the manner of gentlewomen."

Smith College is an American women's liberal arts university at Northampton, Massachusetts. It is named after its founder, Sophia Smith. Smith girls "do not know how to conduct themselves in the manner of gentlewomen", according to Mrs. Ramson. And they have "imbibed some strange modern ideas".

"Yes," I said, "I think I understand."

"Well, Eric," she continued, looking me directly in the eyes, "I hope that to-morrow morning I may look into your eyes and find them just as clear and frank as now. I know you are not going to disappoint me now, are you... dear?"

I mumbled a "No, ma'am," and "Goodbye," and fled the room.

XXXIV

The assembly hall, for the Vladmimir de Pachmann concert, was, due to the effective advertising, no doubt, packed to capacity. Many of the townspeople were there, and the professors with their wives, always in the same evening gowns. Mrs. Ramson was in the balcony with Myron, dressed in her black velvet with the cap, for since Jessie's memorable afternoon in Otterby she had made a tradition of wearing the cap when there was "music in the air." She loved to go about humming that song about the house, always off key: "There's music in the ai-yer, lalalala, la, la, la," or snatches of Scotch "skirls," or that Christmas song, "In green feliciteece."

To go to a concert was a rare thing for the Ramsons, but, of course, when a famous man like De Pachmann came they would have to go if only to be au courant.

The great red curtain of the stage was down, a thing unheard of for a concert, but it was whispered about that the maestro had wished it so. Usually the curtain was hung up in graceful folds at the side, but once, at a students' political rally where a famous Follies girl and a senator spoke, the curtain was drawn down rapidly, for the wisecrackers of the Third Party (this was at the time of the notorious Teapot Dome Scandal) had made a huge backdrop inscribed very simply:

GAS! OIL! PETROLEUM!

and it nearly ruined the evening.

The Teapot Dome Scandal nearly ruined an evening at the Dartmouth Assembly Hall.

XXXV

The talking stopped momentarily as the curtain went up, revealing a grand piano in solitary majesty before a grey curtain. Mr. MacWhoog paused at the door in back and then strode in to his place, causing a number of people to rise from their seats while he passed to his own. No sooner was he seated, however, and everyone ready to see De Pachmann come out, than the rich boy entered with his twenty-four friends all in evening clothes, and their march down to the front rows was nothing less than a parade. It caused a real flurry and Mr. MacWhoog looked annoyed.

At last, after several more moments of taut waiting, the maestro appeared, a bent old man with a curious sidling gait. He went straight for the piano in a beeline, and started playing some chords before he sat down. This took everyone by surprise, and then, just as he seemed ready to sit down and start in earnest, he suddenly wheeled about and, posing with one elbow on the side of the piano, began a long harangue in pidgin English about how well his wife played Debussy.

Vladimir de Pachmann posed with one elbow on the side of the piano and "began a long harangue in pidgin English about ... Debussy."

The audience laughed appreciatively, for they had expected he would do this thing, and then he broke off and almost ran from the platform. He returned with his secretary and a few sheets of white paper a moment later, and paid great attention to the secretary as that man placed the paper underneath one of the legs of the piano chair.

Once more De Pachmann installed himself before the keyboard, and this time he really began. Mrs. Ramson leaned back in her seat, whispering ecstatically to Myron, "Oh, Huneker was right! It is 'hot pearls on velvet!'"

The pianist kept changing his expressions of feature, each one more amazing than the last, while the boys in evening dress, representing the chic aesthetic group of students, looked at each other with rhapsodic smiles. One of them, who wrote numberless sonnets with Greek titles, reached over and took a program from one of his friends, put on his shell-rimmed glasses, took out his fountain pen, assumed the god, and began writing at a furious pace as though he were entranced. Other students looked solemnly from him to the mumbling pianist, actually to see this rare double manifestation of genius before their own eyes! Oh, it was an evening for the aesthetes!

De Pachmann's success was tremendous, and Mrs. Ramson, after talking all the next day about him said that his concert was a "wonderful spiritual 'lift," and finally clinched all encomiums by announcing that "Chopin was to music what Barrie was to literature."

The young Richmond Lattimore (who later became a famous Greek translator and classical scholar) was half of the "double manifestation of genius" at the Vladimir de Pachmann recital, writing as if entranced, and assuming the appearance of a Greek god.

XXXVI

But I was talking about Jessie Tyler. She lived in a most beautiful way, but, of course, that only made it all the more difficult to live in the town and maintain the social connections she had started out with. I was with her a great deal, but I was not in the least in love with her. She did not find any of the young unmarried professors very interesting, but, of course, according to the town traditions, they were the only masculine company she could accept to be seen with in public, and as she preferred a student it was thought very queer and talk began to float around about us. I took her to my fraternity dance and we had a good time, for the jazz was perfect. I was a little worried, though, for it was the first time I had had an out-and-out break with Mrs. Ramson and I wondered how the affair was going to be mended up.

But the funniest part of the whole affair was Mrs. Rosenkrantz. Shortly after the recital that Jessie gave in the Little Theatre, Mrs. Rosenkrantz gave a party for her where she played also, and I was invited.

I went because I wanted to hear Jessie play. She had promised to play some Ravel I had never heard, and as I knew Mrs. Rosenkrantz's affairs were always impossibly mixed, I thought this was to be a town-professor-student kind of party, and was rather surprised to find out I was the only student invited.

As Jessie was taken up with the guests most of the time, I talked with Mrs. Marsh for a while and with Mr. Moorhead, who lived on the other side of the hall from the Rosenkrantzes, and then remained quietly in the corner, out of the way of the people and Mrs. Rosenkrantz, who was amiably threading herself in and out of the crowd making compliments to everybody and saying that Jessie was such an "original" violinist.

After the music we all adjourned to the dining room, where there was a resplendent silver samovar. The tea was served in glasses, and there were all kinds of cookies and a little "original" dainty of Mrs. Rosenkrantz's, candied carrots. I had already made arrangements with Jessie to see her home, so when Colonel Steinlich came up to ask whether he might have that privilege, she told him quite simply that she had already accepted to go with me.

The Colonel looked at me with the kind of exasperation he frequently expressed more violently at the ski jump, merely saying "Oh?" and as he bowed he clicked his heels rather more smartly than usual. Mrs. Rosenkrantz, who had watched this little scene from the doorway, gave me that mysterious smile again, and when I left with Jessie she rushed to open the door for me and whispered triumphantly, "Bravo!"

I was completely mystified, and told Jessie, when we were outside, what had happened.

"Oh, Eric," said Jessie, "she's a strange person! I certainly didn't know what I was in for when I came here to live! But I am not going to let these gossipy people spoil my days."

The significance of Mrs. Rosenkrantz's remark to me was made clear, however, about a week later. I received a written invitation from her to attend a "big Russian tea," and was told that there would be music. Furthermore, she telephoned Mrs. Ramson please to let me go, and Mrs. Ramson told me it was a social duty (we were in accord then after a three days' feud, but that will take up another chapter) and that it would be impolite to refuse since Mrs. Rosenkrantz was of much greater social significance in the town than I and was really bestowing "a signal honour" on me merely because I had played the violin so beautifully at her tea. I said it didn't make any difference to me one way or the other, and went.

To my surprise the only other person there was Jessie, and I wondered if I had mistaken the day. But no, Mrs. Rosenkrantz said, "I just wrote 'big tea' so that you wouldn't be scared away. You know, I have watched your little romance since the first day you met Jessie" Jessie was aghast and I almost open-mouthed. Mrs. Rosenkrantz continued: "And I have been so angry at the people who have said unpleasant things about you, and I know how hard it might be for you to meet one another, so I have made this tea for you in the little dining room, where you can be cozy and all alone, to talk to your hearts' content." Then she smiled very sweetly as she opened the door of the dining room and made us the motion to enter. We sat down in silence at the two plates, both very self-conscious. Mrs. Rosenkrantz remained at the door, and then, with even a greater measure of benevolence, said while closing it, "Lovers can have always a sanctuary at Mrs. Rosenkrantz's."

Jessie poured the tea solemnly, her face expressing mixed feelings. "For goodness' sake, don't laugh," she whispered to me, for I was almost at the end of my self-control; "I'm sure she's watching at the keyhole. Oh, but she is a strange person!"

XXXVII

The day after I returned from the fraternity there was a heavy, cold atmosphere in every room at Otterby. Mrs. Ramson was angry. Not only at me, but at the world in general. It was the beginning of the month and all kinds of bills had arrived, many more than expected, and Delia knew that they would have to get a new car soon, too, for the old Reo was unbelievably shabby.

"The old Reo was unbelievably shabby."

I was always very careful as to the time when I approached Mrs. Ramson for the money on my extra hours. I remember the first time I did it incorrectly: Delia had just made a large payment on the house, and then I arrived with my bill for ten dollars.

"I don't understand this, Eric," Mrs. Ramson said frigidly. "Twenty-five hours of work makes ten dollars at the rate we agreed upon, but I don't see how you have worked twenty-five hours extra for me in the past two weeks. What does this mean?

21 hours for teas
4 hours extra cleaning on Saturday mornings
25 hours, at $.40 = $10.00.

"It surely doesn't take you more than half an hour a day for the actual serving of tea? That's not logical."

"For the actual serving, no," I replied, "but you must realize that that half hour is spread over an hour and a half when I have to be waiting Johnny-on-the-spot in the kitchen."

"Oh, but you can be studying during the intervals," said Delia. "No, I can't consider that working time."

"And then," I continued, "during those intervals I often play the violin for you."

"But, Eric," said Mrs. Ramson in a surprised, hurt tone of voice, "you surely don't want to be paid for that! That's just a nice thing to do in return for the nice things I do for you. You remember I excused you to go to that special afternoon concert, and that day we had so many guests and it was so difficult for me but I never said anything; then, last Sunday morning, I deprived the greatest man in the world of an extra portion of strawberries in order to give you a taste and also the feeling of really being a member of our family, and at every dinner you've served I've given you a canapé of caviar, and I can assure you there are precious few boys here who have such advantages. I've taught you the art of dining and entertaining well, which you can't learn in college; you have heard English beautifully spoken and pronounced ever since you have been here, and you still have need to listen carefully, and I should think just the fact that you can live in such a lovely house as Otterby, with all its cultural advantages, would be enough to make you want to play every afternoon out of sheer joy!"

"At every dinner I've served you a canapé of caviar."

"I'm sorry we look at the question from such different angles," I said, "but if you refuse to give me the amount I still think is just, how much will you give me?"

"This time, of course, you have taken me unawares, and naturally I am forced to pay you the ten dollars," she said, writing out the cheque, "but I will think over tonight how we can best arrange this affair, for I cannot be paying out ten dollars here and ten dollars there every day, for my little fortune would be quite exhausted at such a rate. You know we have undergone heavy expenses recently," she continued, "and all the members of the family must economize."

"Thank you," I said, pocketing the check.

The next afternoon I was called into her bedroom, where she had her "household desk", a small spinet desk with many pigeonholes stuffed to the brim with papers of all kinds. Every once in a while Delia would get these streaks of economy and would construct elaborate budgets and puzzle over all kinds of accounts. This day she presented me with a handsome notebook which she herself had gone to the town in the morning to buy. The notebook was inscribed on the cover, with her large, flowing hand, "Eric's Book," and inside she had carefully dated and numbered all the pages. On the first page she had written a list of my duties:

Furnace	10 min.
Dusting in Drawing and Dining Rooms	12
Sweeping "e cc "c " (twice weekly)	10
Hearth (cleaning and laying fire)	5
Mopping (daily)	18
a. Drawing Room	
b. Dining Room	
c. Hall and Stairs	
Kitchen Floor Washing (twice weekly)	17-20
Bin Emptying (twice weekly)	7
Tea	25
Chopping Wood	
Misc.	

"Now, I want you to copy this list daily," she said, "and put after each duty just how many minutes you have worked. The furnace should not take you more than ten minutes; that is the maximum. If it is eleven, it is because you have been too slow; if it is nine, I know you will be honest enough not to steal a mere minute from me and will faithfully mark "9". You must work briskly when you work, for that is the only way. With the kitchen floor I have given you a leeway of three minutes, as I expect you to do the little hallway only once a week, so that sometimes it will take you twenty, sometimes seventeen minutes. I have gone through the entire list of duties myself and I am sure my figures are exact. Mr. Ramson told me about the furnace and I think his figure is quite a generous one. When the season changes there will be other duties, of course, to take the place of winter activities: gardening and spraying and hanging the awnings."

Oh, I remember when at the autumn we had to take the awnings down! Mrs. Ramson disliked them, as she said they disturbed the rhythm of the lines of the house and were in the summer only a "necessary excrescence." The house had beautiful lines but it was not constructed to take down awnings easily. Barton put them up and he said to me, "I'll be out of town when they have to come down. God, what a hell of a job!" The awnings on the back of the house, which, on account of the hill slant, was four stories high, were most difficult, as the ladder was so flimsy and shaky; every time I leaned over to unscrew a bolt it would totter and shake, and Delia, who was superintending from below, would cry out ineffectively, "Oh, Eric, be careful!"

We got the awnings down just in time that year, for there was a heavy snowfall at the beginning of October, and Clarence, who detested the snow, became very gloomy. It was only the Sunday after he and Jane were for tea at the Feltridges', whose house overlooked the wide expanse of the fairway of the town's golf course, then white and glittering, and Mrs. Feltridge, who with her husband was a great winter-sport fan - they spent their Christmas vacation skiing over the mountains - said wasn't the snow "too beautiful."

The Feltridges' house overlooked the Hanover golf course.

Clarence answered that if it were the middle of August and he were in the middle of the Sahara, by a powerful stretch of the imagination he might be tempted to call snow beautiful, and this unfaithful remark - for the members of the community were supposed to be passionate for skiing, if not in practice, at least in principle - was received with affronted silence.

But I was talking about Mrs. Ramson being angry. The lists I made were an awful bother, but as the book was kept in the kitchen cupboard and inspected regularly for a long while, I had to do them. Gradually, however, Mrs. Ramson forgot to look and I began to do them every other day, and then every three days. For fairly long periods of time Mrs. Ramson, like a barometer, would register fair and warmer, and the work went on smoothly, and I was given delicacies to eat, and introduced to people, even to Robert Frost, as a "member of the family," and then suddenly there would be these catastrophes like calling Jessie by her first name, or the income tax, and Otterby would be a frigid household, and everything I did was wrong, and, of course, always just before these outbreaks I was particularly in good with Mrs. Ramson, and naturally I would get a little careless in my work, for nothing was ever said. And then, the day after the fraternity dance, Mrs. Ramson called me into the drawing room.

"Eric," she began, "have you no sense of amour-propre? Have you no pride in your work? Now, just look at the condition of this hearth. I can't pay you for this kind of work. Why, it's slovenly. Look at this". She pointed to a thin grey line of dust which showed I had not moved the Oxford chair in my mopping. "The one thing a housekeeper cannot bear to have is a filthy hearth. This morning Mrs. Finckner paid me a visit to get a recipe for my sherbert, and she stared at the hearth and at me. Her looks spoke volumes. And I can't tell you how ashamed I was. And still I was loyal to you; I did not say, "This hearth is Eric's work,' for there could only then be the question, "Why do you keep such an inefficient servant? I really don't know why, Eric, I had faith in you once, but I'm beginning to think you are just careless and, what is worse, without pride in your work."

I mumbled something about being sorry and doing better in the future, but Mrs. Ramson was not one to let an advantage slip by so easily. "Just after Mrs. Finckner, Mrs. Beebe came in with a chocolate cake, and you know how disagreeable I find it to be placed in an embarrassing position with such a woman. She just looked at the hearth and the windows and said, 'Humph,' in that rude Omaha manner of hers, and I had to excuse myself as best I could. Now, these windows can't wait another day. Are you going to be busy this afternoon?"

Her tone of voice warned me that I had better not be busy, so I said "No," and spent the afternoon on the windows. The windows were imported from England, made to open outwards, and in little leaded squares, the lead painted black, and as the windows were new there were little black spots of paint on the glass that came off only with alcohol and much elbow grease. There were four big windows in the drawing room, and I was tired when I was done just before tea time.

Mrs. Ramson looked at the windows critically and without much enthusiasm. "This will do," she said. "We will have to wash the windows often, as I simply can't bear that Mrs. Beebe's saying 'Humph' - these Western people are so unpleasant."

"Oh, I made some chicken pâté sandwiches for tea to-day," continued Mrs. Ramson. "There is one waiting for you on a plate in the breakfast nook."

"Thank you," I said. The sandwich was good, but I realized that the storm clouds were still in the sky and that I had better watch my step. The next morning I got up early and did my work with the utmost care, but the moment I stepped into the house on returning, I felt something was wrong.

"Eric!" Mrs. Ramson's voice was sharp. "I don't know what to do with you. I treat you kindly, I feed you on delicacies, I give you all the cultural advantages of my home, I defend you before friends who almost ask, 'Why do you keep such an inefficient servant? and with all this you have no pride in your work and do it carelessly."

"What is wrong?" I asked a little wearily. "I did my work with extreme care this morning."

"The fire was not laid correctly," said Delia; "you must follow a plan in that as well as everything else." I followed her into the drawing room. The sticks were as I had laid them in the morning, with the paper crumpled under them and the big log in back.

"My fires have always burned," I said.

"Yes, but they look too haphazard," Delia said, kneeling down with difficulty before the fireplace and completely demolishing my work, throwing the kindling helter-skelter all over the orange-tiled hearth. "First you must take a look at your kindling and put the smallest and thinnest pieces in front." After much choosing and arranging, she placed two thin strips at a forty-five degree angle from the floor, one end of each touching the andiron. "Then a little bit bigger and a little bit longer," she said, continuing to lay the strips as if she were weaving a basket; "and you must not listen to Myron Ramson on the subject of fires, for he feels honour-bound to use as little kindling as possible and he is very much chagrined if he has to light more than one match. But don't listen to him," she repeated, arranging the sticks so that their angles were exactly even one end with another, "but always use twice as much kindling as you think you need, and lots of paper," she added; "only you must not take double sheets, as you have done, but half sheets of newspapers". She smoothed the sheets I had crumpled, and tore them in half as precisely as possible, and then recrumpled them into neat little snowballs, which she placed in a rough kind of pattern under the wood. "And, lastly, you must choose three larger pieces of wood. These you have are all of a size, and they should rather be proportioned, one a little bit thicker than the other, so that there will be a progress and a rhythm in the fire the same way as in a bar of music. If everything is done precisely and with its inherent rhythm, our lives will subconsciously be influenced for the best, and consequently our outward lives will be more beautiful."

In the last few moments, seized by this new philosophic truth, she had expanded and warmed like the real Delia she was, but then she remembered she was really scolding me and said, a little harshly, "Will you please hurry to get the three pieces of wood, proportionately related to one another, each one a little thicker and bigger than the last?"

"You must get three larger pieces of wood."

When I came with the wood from the cellar, she sent me back again for two logs to be placed at the side of the fireplace. "This is a new ruling," she said, "and I want it to be strictly carried out. I timed you while you were gone, and it took you forty-five seconds, but I will give you fifteen seconds extra, so that you can add one minute to your hearth duty, making six the maximum. Is that understood?"

"Yes, Mrs. Ramson," I answered.

"Before you go, Eric," she continued, "I wish you would empty the bins. I know tomorrow is the day, but they are smelling to heaven and you must tend to them right away."

"They are smelling to heaven and you must tend to them right away."

XXXVIII

The bins were one of Mrs. Ramson's pet household ideas, and acted as a catchall for papers, strings, cans, jars, bottles, and all the other waste products, except garbage, of the kitchen. The papers were supposed to be thrown in the right-hand side, and the bottles and cans in the left, but in the confusion that always existed in the preparation of a big dinner, papers and cans were thrown in whatever bin was handiest, and in cleaning them out I had to separate the two, as the rag-pickers of the town were very particular and would not take papers and bottles mixed; it was a filthy job.

The garbage was disposed of in a can in the corner of the Spanish courtyard, and the can was another bother, for if I was the slightest bit careless and did not slam the cover on tightly, one of the town dogs (there were fourteen wild ones, lanky, yellow mongrels with flappy, yellow ears, cherished by the students, as they were at times able, with their protracted, melancholy baying, to break up boresome lectures) would overturn the can in order to select the choicest morsels, and what was left was impossible to clean up completely, and Mrs. Ramson called it "fertilizer" and kept out of the courtyard. But before I talk about the courtyard, I want to tell you that nice story about the town dogs.

They had carte blanche, of course, in all the classrooms. The college, constantly copying Oxford, had to have traditions, and by common consent it was a tradition not to hinder the dogs from entering where they would, usually in groups of two or three, and they almost ruined William Jennings Bryan's anti-evolution lecture by howling, only that agile penseur scored another ten points by turning to a biology professor and saying, "Do you count these protesters among your distant cousins?"

Oh, the Bryan lecture was a scream; the whole town was in arms over the evolution question for three days at all the street corners, though in all the college he made only one convert. "When I asked Eric," Mrs. Ramson would recount at the dinner table, "if Bryan had convinced anyone that he was right, Eric held up his long musician's finger and said solemnly, 'One.'" Mrs. Ramson enjoyed the lecture hugely, following the strange peregrinations of the silver tongue with audible and ill-timed merriment, much to the disgust of the Baptist grocer and his wife who sat in front of her drinking in the words of wisdom with a reverential attitude. Bryan spoke in a husky voice with seeming sincerity, but all his reasoning power was in ridicule; he started by a savage attack on the college paper's editorial which began, "When you go to hear Bryan to-night, do not check your intelligence at the door with your hat," stressing how much intelligence was necessary in order to combat the evil academic influence on every hand, but he scored his first success in the lecture when he said flatly that Darwin stated we had descended directly from the monkeys and asked if anyone denied the statement. Immediately a young biological instructor who smoked huge cigars in the morning and tried to curry favour among the students by sprinkling his lectures with such remarks as "Now, this dinosaur for actual vegetable consumption was the cat's pajamas," jumped up, saying defiantly, "I do."

"I can always find one in an audience," said Bryan, laughing lightly, and in the stamping of approval that followed (the students were much more given to stamping feet than to clapping hands) continued calmly with his lecture. But it was at the end that he scored his greatest coup. In the general discussion the long, sour Scotch Professor Dundee said, "Have you ever read Frazer's 'Golden Bough,' Mr. Bryan?" Mr. Bryan replied that he had not, whereat Dundee continued, "I regret that my professorial salary does not permit me to buy you a copy, for it would do you good to read it."

"My dear sir," said Byran, walking over to him and ostentatiously presenting him with three ten-dollar bills, "buy me the book and buy a Bible for yourself."

Dundee was so angry he simply got red, and so tongue-tied he could only splutter, while the students, who from the beginning had not taken Bryan seriously, as the professors did, roared with approval.

William Jennings Bryan (died July 26, 1925, not long after his speech), the famed "silver-tongued orator" who ran for President of the United States three times unsuccessfully, and was a leading opponent of Darwin's Theory of Evolution, was interrupted in his speech by the howling of Dartmouth's fourteen wild dogs.

But I was talking about the town dogs. One day, in one of the classrooms, the dogs were particularly obstreperous, and the professor - I think it was old Professor Finckner - decided to put a stop to any further interruptions of a like nature by having passed, at a meeting of the Town Improvement Society, a measure to the effect that all the dogs in the town not muzzled were to be shot. The day after the measure was passed -some of the students got wind of it, and every one of the mongrels was perfectly muzzled but in such a state made more of an uproar than ever, so that the measure had to be repealed as being the greater of two evils.

Free us!

XXXIX

The Spanish courtyard, which was also a souvenir of the sojourn in Brazil, was not the success it was planned to be, as it was on the north side of the house and was always damp. It was not really a courtyard, for it lacked a wall, the rear one, but Mrs. Ramson said if you turned your back to that space, which was occupied mostly by one end of Cedar Pond, you would think you were really in a courtyard. The house and the garage made up two of the walls, connected by the third, which had the grilled wooden garden gate. The gate never completely satisfied Mrs. Ramson, as it was studded with nails,. Alas, Mr. Barton did the studding "so haphazardly; if he had only waited a day, I would have shown him a simple Gothic pattern which would have made the gate perfect." But the chief delight of the courtyard for Mrs. Ramson was the balcony which over hung the side door of the house, which was copied after one of an old Portuguese house and made in carved wooden panels. It was just at the level of the landing of the stairs inside, and the window there opened like a door. Mr. Barton said the balcony was a pretty decoration, but "if Delia ever goes out to stand on it, good-by balcony."

The Ramsons (ie. the Lambuths) lived at the south end of Occum Pond which runs beside the road called Occum Ridge, which is lined with large distingusihed houses. In the book these are called Cedar Ridge and Cedar Pond. Delia's Spanish Courtyard had no north wall, but instead bordered upon Occum Pond.

For a long time after the house was finished the garage was not plastered in colours like the house, for the foundation plaster, due to the wet and cold autumn weather, refused to harden, so that the colour coat could not be applied. The Ramsons used the same system of plastering as the houses of Naples; Myron had talked with the people there to learn the secrets of their wonderful colouring, and naturally, as the garage made up a wall of the courtyard and was grey, while the other wall and the house were of the soft rose colour with all its mad splashes of green and blue and purple and red, it spoiled the courtyard and was a thorn in the flesh of Delia, who wanted Otterby to be perfect inside and out.

Consequently, though the workmen said the garage should not be plastered until spring, when the sun would be more frequent and warmer, Delia said she could not think of entertaining another famous guest, - this time it was Rebecca West, - with the garage in that unfinished condition, so the workmen were hauled off the job they were occupied with at the moment, the erection of an extreme de luxe fraternity house; and Mrs. Ramson was so happy once more to have workmen about, because, she said, they had a sounder philosophy than the philosophy professors, and it gave her that mediaeval feeling of a lady in her castle to have workmen in stone and plaster about the house. She even went to the extent of offering two of them who had shown some friendliness to the dog (most of the workmen detested Scarot) dainty chicken pâté sandwiches, which to her horror they gulped down at one bite.

Since there were workmen about, Mrs. Ramson let Scarot stay out of doors, for he took an evident enjoyment in leisurely watching the men hard at work. It was late autumn but there was an abnormal warm spell at the time, and Scarot stretched out full length on the stones, and even remembered his youth to the extent of chasing a mouse to a hollow in a pile of rocks, and spent the rest of the day, not even deigning to eat at noon, watching the blank hole. "Did you ever see such a dumb cur?" said one of the workmen to me; "watching the hole all day and never paying the slightest attention to us here!" He threatened darkly, "One of these god-damned nights I'm going to come here with my long table knife, and I'll slit that god-damned cur up the guts, - damned if I don't!"

"That would be interesting," I said, thinking where Scarot slept at night.

"Yes, and at the same time," continued the workman, "I'll slit that picture in the downstairs parlour. I call it a disgrace to a house I had a hand in building."

The picture was a copy of Michelangelo's "Adam."

XL

Miss Rebecca West had a cool voice but she made a mistake in wearing pearls, for her skin was tan and flaky and the combination was not pleasant in candlelight. She was the first, last, and only woman celebrity to be received in Otterby while I was there, for Mrs. Ramson was extremely wary of creatures of that genre. "I can't understand how men are so fond of these glittering, brilliant women," she said. Besides, Mrs. Ramson felt a woman's place was in the home at housewifely pursuits. "I can understand how a gentlewoman could write a charming book or paint china or even dabble in water colours, but to write a troubling, serious book like 'The Return of the Soldier' and besides", she whispered to me in the pantry while I was preparing the caviar canapés (Miss West's invitation was Myron's doing alone), "what kind of woman is it that would take for a nom de plume the name of that wretched character of Ibsen's? Oh, no, Eric, it's for men to write books and women to feed them and be charming," and she felt more than ever justified in her opinion when she caught rumours of Fannie Hurst's famous party in New York for the English authoress.

The dinner proceeded at a brilliant pace, for Miss West felt Mrs. Ramson's enmity and was extremely sweet and disarming and haughty with her, which set Mrs. Ramson's teeth on edge, as she did not know how to attack politely then; and Miss West, in her simple white gown, which she wore totally without chic - "English women always wear evening gowns like sports costumes," said Delia, who had given up chic years ago but could still detect the lack of it unerringly in others - kept on directing her attention to Myron, retailing vividly all the gossip of literary London, which so entranced him that he kept on putting more and more of an English accent in his responses, making me feel like a butler more than ever.

Rebecca West "felt Mrs. Ramson's enmity and was extremely sweet and disarming and haughty with her, which set Mrs. Ramson's teeth on edge."

"The Grand Concourse of New York," said Miss West, "thrilled me much more than the Champs-Élysées, though I was taken aback at first by the presumption of the name."

"Oh, New York!" said Myron with repressed ecstasy.

"It is certainly one of the architectural wonders of the world," broke in Professor Wadman heavily, "but I shouldn't care to live there. Now, Constantinople ..."

"Oh, tell us your wonderful 'droshky' story again!" exclaimed Delia brightly to Professor Wadman. Mrs. Ramson used the word "droshky" because she said the story, which was about an adventurous ride in a Turkish carriage, gave her "a Russian feeling", but Professor Wadman was too slow getting under way and Miss West had already launched into the subject of American advertising.

"Advertising," said Myron impressively, "just fails being an art. It employs all the literary effects of a fine poem. I mean it is highly suggestive; it is composed, it has form, construction often more rigid than a sonnet, but inasmuch as it is not an expression of man's spiritual life, it fails as an art."

"Some of the phrases are marvellously ingenious," said Miss West, "for instance, one I saw advertising for advertising: 'Tell it to Sweeney; the Stuyvesants will understand."

At this point in the dinner Miss West dropped her handkerchief on the floor, but only I saw it and, of course, I immediately picked it up, and she took it so mechanically and so under cover that I felt she might have dropped it on purpose to pull off that very American line from a current musical comedy: "And it still works, it still works..." but she said nothing, not even "Thank you."

When I came back into the room with the sherbert, conversation had turned to winter sports.

"Skiing always seemed to be to be a spectacular way of committing suicide," said Myron, "though it rarely happens that we have accidents even on the big jump."

> "Skiing always seemed to be a spectacular way of committing suicide," said Myron.

"Our whole family," said Delia, "is very fond of skiing. Of course, I am an invalid". Miss West looked particularly solicitous. "And I never stir from the house in the winter, but Myron is ardent for the sport."

"Not the jumping, my dear," said Myron. "Cross-country, however, is rather agreeable."

As a matter of fact, Myron did very little skiing; indeed, his skiing might be called an annual affair, for it was rarely more than once in the season that he ventured forth, usually on the day of the big ski jumps, when everyone would be on the paths. Myron knew that an interest in sports inspired student respect, but he really did like football and never missed a game in the season.

After the dinner was over, I heard Miss West talking to Mrs. Ramson at the "heart of the house" in the hall. She had been saying admiring things about the house, and then I listened with wide-open ears.

"That butler of yours, where did you pick him up, in England?" she asked.

"Oh, no, he's just a lad from Chicago," said Mrs. Ramson. "He uses Barrie's 'Admirable Crichton' for a butler's handbook, and we think he gets on rather well."

"I am more and more amazed at your country," said Miss West. "I never knew that such an intelligent servant class existed."

Rebecca West "never knew such an intelligent servant class existed" in America.

XLI

As Miss West left the same night, or rather on the early morning train, she never got a real look at the outside of the house, which was expressly vexing to Mrs. Ramson, as the garage had been finished to no good use and against Myron's wishes, who, moreover, triumphed by saying that the work had been done so hastily it was not correct and the whole process would have to be gone through again the following spring, naturally at the same expense.

"Inviting her was your doing, my dear," said Mrs. Ramson, "and I had to have the house in order. You may be sure that if I did not have the garage in order, Miss West would have stayed to see it, and I don't want Englishwomen to have an inferior idea about American housekeepers."

"My dear, my dear," said Myron, waving his hands in slight annoyance, "you are exaggerating," and he walked into his study and closed the door.

As the subject of Rebecca West always had a ragged edge, Mrs. Ramson refused to read her new novel, "The Judge", on the ground that it "would surely be too grim for pleasant reading", and when it was announced that Edna St. Vincent Millay was coming, Mrs. Ramson was strangely deaf to the hints of the president of the Arts Club about the entertainment of Miss Millay while she was in the town, and did not even go to hear the lecture.

Jane, who had returned from a visit in Virginia, and Myron went, though Jane said that the woman had really too much fortune: to be born with a name like that and then marry into another one so beautiful (what was it, Boissevain? – I remember Keith Preston suggested that the man receive an honorary degree from Vassar, as Miss Millay was his second or third wife from that institution of learning), and that she thought her sonnets were really too involved.

They went like hordes of others, for the poet at that time was enjoying a tremendous collegiate vogue, members of the more esoteric coteries lisping her numbers on every possible occasion, but they went only to be disappointed, for neither the poet nor her husband turned up until late that night, claiming they had pushed the Ford farther than the Ford had carried them, and the whole town was agog the next morning at the story that Edna (everyone called her Edna then) had not eaten at the fashionable hotel but in the lowest of the student hash houses and there, surrounded by a group of wide-eyed lads, talked so much that her husband at length set his back resolutely to the most audacious listeners and addressed his wife: "For God's sake, Edna, shut up and eat!"

Edna's husband Eugen Jan Boissevain got fed up and said: "For God's sake, Edna, shut up and eat!"

But they had had many happier occasions.

XLII

The lecture was held in the Little Theatre the next afternoon at four, and it was packed with an impatient and curious crowd. Suddenly, after a long wait, she appeared magically in the aisle, following Bob Merlton, the Arts Club president. She was dressed in a dark blue serge dress, with the skirt heavily embroidered in flowers of the same colour, and over her shoulders, in a romantic gesture, was thrown a violently yellow Spanish scarf.

On the platform she looked extremely timid and frail, which impression was augmented by a slight cough in the beginning of her reading. The cave-man protective instinct of every man in the audience was roused, and they were all sympathetically inclined to her anyway.

Before she began speaking she took off her shawl and nonchalantly threw it over the high backed Italian Renaissance speaker's chair, making an immediate and vivid stage setting for her little play, "Two Slatterns and a King."

Old Mrs. Finckner, on hearing the word "slattern," felt all her suspicions concerning Edna were realized, and did not wait to hear any more, and caused a great deal of disturbance leaving, as she had been seated in the middle of a row rather far front. Miss Millay looked after her with some wonderment, and then, putting her head on one side slightly, her large pale eyes carefully adjusted to be just over the heads of the audience, she began reading in a low, restrained voice. There was no applause when she finished, only a holy silence and a wind of gentle smiles and nods.

The high point of the lecture was reached, however, near the end-the boy who wrote sonnets with Greek titles nearly swooned, while some of the ladies followed after her, whispering the lines to themselves-when her voice began rising and falling in augmented thirds to the tune of
"We were very tired, we were very merry,
We had been riding back and forth all night on the ferry."

The thrill in the audience, however, was due to the fact that the poem was supposed to be telling a true story: of arriving too late before the closed, disapproving gates of Vassar and so spending the night by aimlessly crossing and recrossing the river.

When Edna St. Vincent Millay appeared for her reading, she "looked extremely timid and pale ... The cave-man protective instinct of every man in the audience was roused". Richmond Lattimore was so overwhelmed that he "nearly swooned".

I remember when Louis Untermeyer came, one of the first questions flung to him was: "What about all these myths attached to Edna St. Vincent Millay?"

Louis Untermeyer insisted that all the "mythical" tales about Edna St. Vincent Millay were actually true.

"Oh, but they aren't myths," said Untermeyer, with an arch of his eyebrows. "That's just the trouble; they're all true."

At the close of the lecture, of course, the poet was enthusiastically applauded, and Edna had a hard time escaping the autograph hunters who came with fountain pens in hand and opened books, pleading with her at every step.

Myron was not very well pleased with the lecture. "'I cannot help thinking," he said, "that there was more of the afflatus in 'Renascence': where she says: 'All I could see from where I stood/ Were three long mountains and a wood.' She has lost that naiveté which was her chief charm, and she has gained nothing by the loss except a shallow, fashionable cleverness."

Mrs. Ramson was even stronger in her denouncement of Edna's work: "Her poems do not read to me as though they were written by a gentlewoman. Perhaps I am mistaking impertinence for candour, but I do know there is a deplorable lack of discretion. When I read that sonnet, 'Oh, World, I cannot hold thee close enough,' I positively blushed, for it is far too intimate a revelation of the soul to be put into such bold words on paper."

The collegiate vogue of Edna held on for a long while nevertheless, until one Sunday the Rev. Dr. Fosdick arrived. He spoke in the late afternoon, a winter vespers service, and the green walls of the chapel were as sour-coloured as the skies outside. The chapel was an ugly place, Romanesque Mansard style, with a useless tower all bevels and niches and arrow slits, containing three of the loudest, most jangling, and ill-tuned bells in America. The president thought that part of the lack of religious interest among the students was due to the forbidding aspect of the chapel and its lack of comfort. The seats were of wood and wicker, and on each one was placed a doleful ticket which had to be signed in order to register attendance. Chapel was compulsory, and the only pleasant thing about it was the organ, which Hampden played that day, a beautiful Bach toccata. Fosdick spoke, and what he said was conservative enough, but his manner was that of a man of the world, which deceived one to listen. And finally, to give a modern fillip to his discourse, he quoted:

"The world stands out on either side
No wider than the heart is wide;
Above the world is stretched the sky,
No higher than the soul is high.
The heart can push the sea and land
Farther away on either hand;
The soul can split the sky in two,
And let the face of God shine through."

The aesthetes shuddered with horror at these lines without knowing who had written them, for they sounded very strange removed from their context, and then, when it dawned that the poet was the beloved Edna, dark suspicions as to her poetry began to rise, for the quotation was far more apt for a sermon than to be used lightly over the teacups.

The Dartmouth Chapel, where 'dark suspicions" about Edna St. Vincent Millay's poetry "began to rise".

XLIII

Billy Sunday had been a famous baseball player, who then turned into a passionate evangelist. He spoke at the Dartmouth chapel before I went to Dartmouth. Myron had not gone to chapel after that unfortunate Billy Sunday meeting, while Mrs. Ramson had been an invalid on Sundays for many years. It seems that when Billy Sunday spoke - I wasn't there then, so I only speak from what I have heard from others - he was a quiet, well-behaved gentleman speaking the King's English and this took everyone by surprise, as it had been expected that the godly ex-pinch-hitter of baseball would lift the roof with holy bombast and startle the professors into retreat with his slang. But no, he spoke quietly and pled so eloquently on the subject of "A Clean Life" that at the end, when he asked all who were in accord with his principles to come forward and shake hands with him, Myron was among the first to do so. But the unfortunate part of the occurrence was the next day, when there were headlines in The Boston Globe and other papers about Myron which said:

ENGLISH PROFESSOR
HITS SAWDUST TRAIL

Billy Sunday preaching with a Bible in his hand.

Billy Sunday could thunder away at any congregation and threaten them with eternal damnation.

But at Dartmouth Billy Sunday was quiet and well-behaved and spoke "the King's English", so Myron shook his hand.

XLIV

About the middle of the year there would be changes in the teaching staff, and as Myron was head of the English Department he naturally had to select new teachers, and he found the best way of examining them was by giving a dinner over which Delia also presided, and it was her dictum usually that decided whether it was thumbs up or down. In all her long experience at this, she made (according to Myron) only two mistakes; one of them was Mr. Shorter, and the other a wild, romantic aviator, Darkney Evans. Mrs. Ramson had a weakness for the military anyway, as her uncle had been a soldier, and she said he was one of the most perfect gentlemen she had ever known. She recalled with tender amusement his polite exasperation when his arm was broken and he could no longer tie his bow tie, at all her attempts to reach his perfection of tying. Darkney Evans never broke his arm, but he flew over Paris during the war and wrote a poem about it which Mrs. Ramson said was "of first water," and then married a brisk, matter-of-fact Parisienne who took to the life of our town bravely but without much enthusiasm. Darkney Evans was one of those extremely disillusioned men who attempt to make life liveable by making it absurd, but who had such a sense of futility about his work that his teaching was dull, and by venting some of his displeasure at the universe by means of giving low marks he received no sympathy from his students.

Just why Darkney was not a success, and indeed was such an unpleasant failure, it was hard to put your finger on. He did not object to his wife's making special cakes and meat pies to sell although she lost on the project, as she used such expensive materials, and then Darkney constructed a still which never worked but caused a slight, embarrassing explosion, and he always just failed at being really chic at the dinner table by demanding a second portion of soup.

But if Darkney Evans did not turn out to be a find, Antony Troy Tarpon certainly rose quickly into high favour with Mrs. Ramson and had all the earmarks of becoming a professor long before his thirtieth year. Mrs. Ramson was enthusiastic over him, and almost immediately dropped Harold MacDarren for this tall young man with a moustache, a swift suave tongue, and a pair of brown eyes which looked straight at you and yet seemed shifty. Mrs. Ramson always had one of the young instructors under her special tutelage so that they could absorb all of Myron's literary and pedagogic principles without tiring out the great man. She would invite the instructor - it was Harold MacDarren for a long time, as he was an invalid and "needed coddling" - for ten 'o'clock breakfasts in the Garden Room, and there, before the roaring fire, with the coffee pot set on a little special stone ledge beside the fireplace so that the coffee would have a "woodsy taste," they would sit and talk with emotion about art and life.

Sometimes Harold would be ill for three days at a time and Mrs. Ramson would lavish every care on him- "The young Keats," she would exclaim, "he can get well just on luxury!" And there would be flowers, and his coffee cup and egg cup would bear the arms of his college at Oxford -- the whole set of them bought by Mrs. Ramson years ago - and caviar and chicken pâté sandwiches. Then Harold, tired of talking, would lean back on the chaise longue to read as I cleaned off the rose-topped breakfast table, or sometimes, more ambitiously, he would sit down in a chair at the piano and play Chopin with faint passion.

It was quite different with Antony Troy Tarpon. Mrs. Ramson said he was "such a man of the world and, compared with Harold, had so much more 'rest' and went so much deeper." He could have played the invalid, too, as he enlisted in the aviation - though he never got across to Europe in wartime - and crashed to ground a month later, hurting an arm and leg so badly that he lost perfect control over the left hand, even tipping a glass of water over into Mrs. Ramson's lap at his first dinner in Otterby, saying suavely, "Excuse me … the war … my hand …" and probably Mrs. Ramson decided that moment that he be hired. "He is a man of experience, a true soldier of fortune"; and she listened breathlessly to the account of his accident and how two weeks after, against the doctor's orders, he forced himself out of bed and used crutches, all in order to attend a sporting date: a crocodile hunt in the Everglades of Florida; and this gentlemanly gesture quite won over Delia.

Then, too, Antony Troy Tarpon was unmarried and had never been divorced and, when discreetly questioned on the subject of marriage, was not evasive, as was Harold, but admitted quite frankly that he had travelled all his life and now wanted to settle down to a quiet home life. All Mrs. Ramson's love of matchmaking was aroused, and she began to plan teas and teas, and by the time young Mr. Antony Troy Tarpon left Otterby that first visit, she had him married to at least three girls of the town and was meditating a fourth.

Unfortunately, Antony Troy Tarpon crashed his plane before he got to Europe and thereafter had imperfect control of his left hand. Mrs. Ramson was so entranced by this "true soldier of fortune" that she made Myron hire him for the English Department.

XLV

Shortly after the advent of Mr. Antony Troy Tarpon, Otterby was plunged into great confusion at a letter from Jane saying she was coming home two weeks sooner than she had planned. Mrs. Ramson called Mrs. Fife over, and all three of us went over the house like a hurricane, sweeping and dusting and washing windows on the inside and waxing the floors and rearranging the furniture till Otterby shone at every corner. And there was much telephoning to the grocery and to the florist; Jane's room was burdened with flowers: tall bending tulips in dull red and yellow, and pale orange sprigs of giroflée. Her room was the prettiest of all the bedrooms, being plastered in pale green and orchid, with the woodwork in an indeterminate shade of orchid-rose. The bed was built in a little alcove, low and covered with a gay-figured muslin to match the curtains, and the dressing table was a dainty oval one that Mr. Barton had made himself. The door was painted green, and on the outer side was painted a little garland of flowers with Shakespeare's words:

"With everything that pretty bin,"

and a little bronze bust of Shakespeare below to act as a door knocker.

The Ramsons had a similar door knocker.

Jane arrived in a flurry of snow, dressed in a black coat trimmed with leopard and a black hat, so chic and detached one might have thought she had just stepped off the Rue de la Paix and was on her way to Rumpelmayer's. She adored Paris, and was as Parisian in her speech, gestures, dress, and thought as any woman born and bred in the shadow of the Faubourg Saint Germain could be. Madame Nechicheff once whispered to me, as Jane was helping her mother serve tea over a little table she had bought in London, with a silver tea service that had belonged to Lady Hamilton - the pot was beautifully fluted and engraved - "Monsieur Eric, voilà une femme avec le urai chic. On ne les voit pas souvent en Amérique."

I learned a lot about Paris from Jane, and I called her Jane, for she told me to, though Mrs. Ramson said that if I would not call her Miss Ramson, which was a bit stiff for an accepted member of the family, I should call her Miss Jane, but as I felt like a railway porter when I addressed her this way, I simply used the 'you' form of address, and when Mrs. Ramson was away I called her Jane.

Mrs. Fife told me that Jane had "gone to Europe a girl and come back a woman"; at any rate, the change that there was, was puzzling to Delia, for she found herself for once without the upper hand, being contradicted elusively and subtly on every side. Mrs. Ramson said that gentlewomen did not smoke in public but (she repeated) "reserved cigarettes for tragic occasions like funerals." Jane calmly continued smoking about the house when she would, especially at tea, with a little ivory cigarette holder that she had bought in Florence, on which was carved an elephant. "Father," she called out once from the study when she was taking some of his store, "I do wish you wouldn't buy these English cigarettes; the Luckies are much easier on my throat."

In the next room Delia quivered and then shut her lips in silence.

"Luckies" were so much easier on Jane's throat.

XLVI

Clarence Rollinson became a regular visitor to the house now after his long absence, but it was evident that Mrs. Ramson had given up the struggle and was trying to make the best of the situation. She spoke a great deal about Mr. Rollinson when he was not there to the tea guests: how he was one of "those rare persons with a brilliant mind and a tender heart", and Professor Ramson continued the propaganda by declaring several times in public that he wished he had more on his staff like Mr. Rollinson. Of course, with Myron there was no sham, for he was really fond of Clarence; the two had written a book on the short story together, and the only point on which they did not agree whole-heartedly was the subject of Japanese poetry. Clarence said it surfeited him so quickly, while Myron replied that he did not have, evidently, the "right conception of the Oriental mind."

'Clarence Rollinson' according to Delia was 'one of those rare persons with a brilliant mind and a tender heart'. His real name was Kenneth Allan Robinson, and here is a photo of him as he was in 1922, the year Bravig Imbs arrived at Dartmouth. He was then Assistant Professor of English. He married 'Jane' (real name Jean) and ended up becoming Head of the English Department, just as her father had been.

Jane was very quiet and reserved about Clarence, but they were together a great deal and there was much serious talking between them. Jane converted Clarence into thinking that Paris was a more agreeable place to live in than London, which was a point in her favour, as London represented a great deal to Clarence.

Mrs. Ramson tried all sorts of ways to pick a quarrel with Clarence pleasantly, for a long time without success, as he was extremely discreet and did not push the advantage he had acquired in the least. He could wait. Finally, however, he became gently irritated at this méchante intention of Delia's and stopped coming for a few days. Jane cried a little, and Mrs. Ramson told me to tell Clarence to come for tea, but he did not, and then Mrs. Ramson learned through Jane that he would not come unless he received a written invitation, and it must have been sent, for he arrived, very late and very elegant, dressed in a fur coat and a pale green tweed suit with a dark green cravat and dark green socks. Mrs. Ramson had told me not to let in a single person, and if they arrived, to tell them that she regretted not seeing them but she was indisposed. So he was the sole guest. Jane had gone over to visit Eloise Snow. Nevertheless, Mrs. Ramson had prepared as if there were twenty guests, with caviar sandwiches in shameful profusion. Clarence was extremely fond of them. There was cinnamon toast and a special peppermint candy he liked also that she had spent the morning making, and after I had served tea Mrs. Ramson told me to prepare a cup for Mr. Ramson when he came in, the inference being that not even he should enter, and that I should close the drawing-room doors "firmly" and continue the directions she had given me in the earlier part of the afternoon.

I stayed in the kitchen to study, for it was warm there and Jane came home early by the kitchen entrance.

"Did he come, Eric?" she said to me anxiously.

"Yes," I answered.

"Oh, Eric!" she exclaimed happily, and went up to her room. When she came down to dinner Clarence stayed; Mrs. Ramson looked worn but happy. She was dressed in a gown she secretly detested but which delighted Delia: a mouse-gray velvet one with long tight sleeves flared at the wrist with rose lining, a wide skirt with a tight bodice and the neck high and buttoned up in the style of the "Divine Sarah" Bernhardt at the epoch when Mrs. Ramson was at once thrilled and scandalized over her.

XLVII

At last everyone in the town knew Jane and Clarence were engaged, and I found some of the ladies of the faculty particularly charming to me, for some of them would have given their eye teeth to know what was going on under the pale roofs of Otterby at that time. But they never knew from me.

About a month after the news of the engagement (always unofficial, of course), Mrs. Ramson suddenly turned to me in the kitchen - she always became emotional over making sandwiches - and said, "Eric, can you keep a secret?"

"As well as most," I replied.

"Will you swear scarlet-blue-crimson' that you'll never tell?"

The oath was a new one to me, but it sounded bloody enough, so I swore by it.

"Jane is going to marry Mr. Rollinson!"

"Oh," I said, "how unexpected and pleasant!"

Mrs. Ramson stared a split of a second at me and then said, looking at the clock, "Gracious, Eric, it's almost four-thirty and I'm not dressed yet! Will you finish up these sandwiches? Just butter them"-she ran to the hall, for the doorbell had sounded, and called back from the stairs, "but not too thickly, or they'll be greazy!"

I opened the door for Mrs. Soccy just as Mrs. Ramson closed her bedroom door upstairs.

XLVIII

When the spring came the Ramsons always went out to see the Doles. The Doles lived some thirty miles up the line on the other side of the river, and their farm was called the Twin Hedges. Mrs. Ramson was particularly anxious to go this year, for the new Reo was particularly resplendent, a state in which it never lasted long, as Myron was not one to monkey around a garage. He treated the machine as he treated himself: straight hard work until it broke down, and then a long vacation.

The Ramsons were fond of motoring but it was not the real automobilist's passion, as Myron rarely went faster than twenty-five miles an hour. Mrs. Ramson liked motoring because the "country looks so like England, roads cross brooks just as they do in that lovely country, and the doorways are so pure in style.' Scarot always accompanied them on their trips and he rarely sat still. The Reo was a closed car, and Scarot would scratch and scream at the windows as though he had never seen windows in his life. Not that he did not enjoy riding.

If for some reason they tried to sneak off on a ride without him, there was no telling what would happen to the house, for, as one of the young instructors said, "Hell hath no fury like that Scarot scorned."

Mrs. Ramson liked to ride far up the desolate roads, during the season, in quest of apple blossoms, for many of the farms were abandoned, and if she was successful the Reo came back chugging slowly, burdened with flowery branches like a float in a country-fair parade.

The car was full of branches of apple blossom taken from the abandoned farms, and looked like a float in a rural parade.

Mrs. Ramson loved to recount, at tea, how up in the desolate hills she would find old farmer women "clinging to the rich philosophy of earth," with whom she evidently had long conversations on subjects ranging from birth to death and the old-fashioned way of pickling cucumbers by rubbing the jars with garlic. This latter bit of wisdom she modified in making the salad: the bowl would be rubbed with a morsel of garlic, and so Mrs. Ramson would exclaim triumphantly at dinner, "You have the taste of garlic without eating it, and none of its ill effects!"

But I was talking about the spring trip to the Doles'. They usually set off an hour or so later than scheduled, about two in the afternoon, and this year Roger Fadden Mote roused himself out of a welter of haiku and went along. Clarence did not go; he said he simply could not bear "that woman. That woman was Mrs. Dole, and if you had stronger nerves than she, her talk and presence were a kind of intoxication. She was a woman of tremendous force, and opening a door was for her a matter of dynamic importance. She walked elastically but not swiftly. What Clarence could not bear about her was her voice, which was not so high-pitched as the impression led one to believe, but which was unpleasantly and evenly intense, whether she was in their pale-panelled drawing room serving flaky waffles with maple syrup or calling her daughter in from canoeing on the little river that ran behind the old house.

The daughter, Ella, was a supple girl of twelve, with shy manners, deep brown eyes, and a glittering, almost Vanity Fair kind of conversation. "A modern nymph of the woodland," Mrs. Ramson called her. There was a son too, considerably older, but he was always in the background. He was at home among the whirling lathes of his carpenter's shop or at the dam where he had transformed the river into a source of power or in the mill where they boiled down the maple sap to syrup and sugar.

The house and the sugar factory (formerly a barn) had never been painted, and the dark brown colour of the wood stood in sharp contrast to the bright white shutters. But the settled feeling of the house was due mostly to Mr. Dole (who rarely appeared when visitors were about), a former landscape gardener. Every tree and bush in Twin Hedges owed its place to his judgment, and Mrs. Ramson said that "the trees were not stationed, but rather knit into the lines of the house, giving the general vista, at the same time, a sense of 'lift' and "rest."

But it was the sunken garden that Delia liked most. The garden had formerly been the foundation of an old smokehouse, and it was about five feet deep, floored and lined with flat granite slabs, the interstices brightly outlined with green grass. There was a stone fireplace at one end and a little toy garden at the other, its forest full of bears and its castle surrounded by soldiers.

Mrs. Ramson liked Mrs. Dole very much. They sat and talked together in the garden, while Jane went off "exploring" with her father and Roger Fadden Mote.

"Clarence couldn't come," said Mrs. Ramson; "he had a headache. I suppose you've heard the news...?"

Later on they had a picnic supper in the sunken garden, and Mrs. Ramson cast off restraint and became absurd and hilarious. She felt she owed it to her wine to become gay, and even went to the extent of demanding Mr. Dole's old tweed hat, which she perched atop her head, and sang a few Scotch "skirls" with Scarot in her lap (he had been busily searching mice all afternoon), and Scarot howled his lustiest before the roaring fire, from which little pieces of flaming tinder shot up straight and high into the night.

XLIX

Those spring mornings I used to get up very early in order to play golf on the links nearby before the crowds came. My room (which Myron said looked like Halloween, for the walls were yellow and the armchair pumpkin coloured) was always very gay in the sun, and there was no difficulty in arising. Of course, I never told Delia about my golf playing, for had she known I could get up at such an hour every day, she would have found other duties to fill out the time.

She did find out one day, however, but in such a manner that the incident was never referred to. For a while, you know, the bathroom which adjoined her bedroom was out of working order, so she used Jane's, which was farther down the hall.

Oh, I will never forget that morning! I slung my bag of clubs over my shoulder and opened the door to the hall just as Delia opened the door of her bedroom. We both stood at opposite ends of the hall at precisely the same moment, but the difference was that I was dressed and Delia did not have a thing on. I was so surprised I could only stare stupidly and exclaim to myself: "What marmoreal limbs!" Delia stared back so horrified she could not move, and there we stood like two frozen statues, the morning sun streaming goldenly on the floor between.

But only for a moment. Crossing her arms over her breasts with a convulsive gesture, Delia fell sidewise against the door and thence into her room with an ear-piercing scream of terror I shall never forget. It so frightened me I rushed to my room and locked myself in; the turning of the lock sounded like a gunshot, for the silence after that scream was fervent and profound.

L

The orbit of Antony Troy Tarpon, to continue the astronomy professor's happy figure, was certainly the most varied and elliptical of anyone in town. You were always meeting him, either on the street or on the campus. He never missed a concert or a lecture, and he was almost as frequent a visitor at Otterby as Clarence. He had a way of slipping into any important collegiate event, and if there were photographs, you would be sure to find him in the first row. I remember when Mrs. Ramson gave a great party for the President; there were forty people and I had two servants besides the Indian maid under me and seven tables to look after. Antony Troy Tarpon managed somehow by pulling strings with Mrs. Ramson a week ahead to be seated at the President's table, and you may be sure he did not waste the opportunity of letting the President know there was a new and brilliant addition to the English Department.

The president talked very little but his presence was decidedly distinguished, one eyebrow, bristly-grey, always arched in cynical interrogation. Mrs. Ramson said the eyebrows were often more reliable guides to character reading than eyes themselves: "Any artist can tell you what capacities for revelation there are in a single line."

The dinner was exceptional, for one of the family laws was broken: the telephone rang: a long-distance call for the President, and on my telling him so he immediately rose from the table, excused himself, and answered it. That was something Myron would never have done, for his dislike of being disturbed while dining mounted almost to a phobia. One of the first things I learned at Otterby was to be perfectly adamant over the telephone. Myron might be only a few yards away calmly dining, but for the unfortunate caller he was simply not at home. Once Professor Curman, the next-door neighbour, telephoned at the sacred hour, and I replied with that chill courtesy which is the butler's prerequisite:

I: "I am sorry, but Professor Ramson is not at home."

P. C.: "Excuse me, but this is Professor Curman talking."

I: "Yes, I understand, I will tell him you called as soon as he comes in."

P. C.: "But he is in. I can see from my study window that he is at dinner."

I: "I am sorry, but I have strict orders not to disturb Professor Ramson until he has finished dining."

P. C.: (testily) "Very well, I will call later."

When coffee was over, Mrs. Ramson called me into the drawing room. "Who called, Eric?" she asked.

"Professor Curman," I answered. "He was slightly annoyed not to have had the communication, as he could see Professor Ramson from his study window."

"Myron!" exclaimed Delia at my answer: "what barbarous people these Yankees are! Seeing you at dinner, and then calmly telephoning! Incredible!"

Mrs. Ramson could become very Southern if the occasion served. I remember at a tea shortly before her parents came to visit her she said to the librarian and young Mr. MacNeil, "Please come to visit me often when Mama and Papa are here, for I want to prove to them that the Yankees are really a sociable people even if they aren't."

But I was talking about Antony Troy Tarpon. He did not long remain unknown on the campus, partly because he allowed "discussions" in class, which meant little more than aimless remarks over nineteen different subjects, and, consequently, postponed assignments; he was a prominent rooter at the basketball games, and allied himself solidly to the red-blooded he-man movement of the college which opposed the cultural inroads of the "aestheets" (as they were dubbed by the Flaming Terrapin), whose principal achievement was the establishment of tea as a legitimate pastime. But his popularity was due mostly to his "evenings at home." As Mrs. Ramson said, he was "a man of experience," and he did not make the mistake Mr. Shorter did of telling dirty stories in class and so being forced to resign, but he proceeded on the same path with different lanterns. His "evenings at home" were devoted to serious discussions of sex, which subject, whether on the light or heavy side, was the only one the students were really interested in. He called his "evenings" to Delia "welfare work" -for it appeared that temptations in college were much stronger and varied than believed and she was thrilled at this "noble sacrifice of his personal time" and warned him that he might be taking too much on his shoulders. But trust Antony Troy Tarpon to overburden himself! His only vice was conversation, and as he indulged it to excess he was continually searching for new subjects. Now he would be seen in his sheepskin coat on some prominent hill, easel against the wind, painting away furiously. Then, for a few weeks, he would talk about painting, brush technique, and the "dynamics of composition," for he had definite pretensions to a deep knowledge of art, whether literary or plastic.

He also wrote carefully articulated sonnets, for, as he explained in class in urging his students to take up verse writing, no man could hope to possess a perfect prose style without a corresponding proficiency in prosody.

After the Easter vacation, though, he was noticeably tired and began to worry that he would be losing the brilliant position he had made for himself in the community. Of course, he was not without resources. One Monday evening, after he had just returned from his home in Boston, he proudly produced an old violin in the drawing room of Otterby after dinner, saying that it had belonged to his grandfather. The dinner had been a meagre one, but Mrs. Ramson had added, at the last minute, an extra dessert course of figs and nuts, served in the red Chinese bowl, saying, "You know, my dear Barrie says, somewhere in one of his last books, that figs and nuts make a dinner a feast."

Antony Troy Tarpon smiled reverently at the name of Barrie, and then went on blandly with his story: how he was searching for some old letters in the attic when he had come on the old violin case and "the dear old fiddle I used to play as a boy."

"You frighten me with your versatility," said Delia. "I can understand your painting, for I draw a little myself, but music has always been a blind spot for me, and that you should have the two gifts seems incredible!"

Antony Troy Tarpon smiled modestly, and delicately plucked the strings, which were sadly out of tune. "Of course, I don't know," he continued, "but I think the violin is quite valuable; they say, you know, the older a violin, the more it's worth. I'm sceptical, but not uncertain that it's a real Stradivarius, for there is a label inside which says "Stradivarius' and a date I can't make out."

Mrs. Ramson called me in to see the violin, and Antony Troy Tarpon regarded me in a very surprised manner as he handed over the instrument, for it was clear he was not accustomed to butlers. It was an ordinary Leipzig fiddle; the varnish had been scraped off the corners and rubbed with fiddler's green to make it seem older than it was. I doubted the attic story very much.

"It is not a Stradivarius," I said; "but a copy; however, it may have a good tone. May I take your bow?"

It was not a Stradivarius.

"Oh, I left the bow at home," said Antony Troy Tarpon. Trust him not to run the danger of playing in case he were asked! So I went upstairs for my own bow and played a little on his violin, but it had a hollow, gluey tone.

"It does sound old," said Mrs. Ramson. "Let's hear you play it, Mr. Tarpon."

"Oh, no! Oh, no!" he answered hastily. "In a month or so, when I'm back in practice, I'll come and give you a concert, but not tonight. Besides... my hand ... the war...."

But at the end of the month the violin was forgotten. He did take a few lessons with Jessie Tyler, but she dropped him finally, as he never practiced. "I can't scold him because he's not a little boy," she said, "but he doesn't work." Meanwhile he would go on blaguing at the Faculty Club how he made progress on his fiddle without practicing and how much fun it was to fool the professor, a sport he had lost sight of since his student days.

The violin was forgotten partly in an effort to divert all his energy towards one sole goal, newly seen. For Mrs. Ramson's carefully engineered teas and matchmaking meditations had borne fruit at last. The goal was Miss Marian Hoard, newly arrived from Detroit, where she had been a social worker with more ardour than nerves and more self-sacrifice than time. Her father, James Hoard, was almost one of the institutions of the college, he had taught archaeology so long there. And yet, unlike the old professors, his classes were not dry and dead but frequently very lively. Once one of the professors went into his classroom during a teaching hour for a request of some kind and found James Hoard lying bellywise on the floor. He looked at the students in surprise and they glared back at him, angry at the interruption.

"What's the matter?" asked the professor in high confusion.

"Nothing, my dear sir," said James Hoard with perfect dignity, also slightly annoyed at the interruption, and not changing his horizontal position. "I am just explaining one of the finer points in the technique of rabbit hunting. Now you take the gun " he said, continuing his discourse.

Professor 'James Hoard' was really Professor George Dana Lord. Here is a photo of him in 1922, the year Bravig Imbs arrived. He was 'almost one of the institutions of the college'. But he was annoyed at being interupted, because: "I am just explaining one of the finer points in the technique of rabbit hunting."

LI

Myron was rarely angry and never peevish, but he did not disbelieve in righteous indignation. I remember one night I came in about nine o'clock by the kitchen way, and Mrs. Ramson must have been watching for me, for she stopped me in the hall with her finger on her lips and said, "Oh, Eric, tread softly; the lion is having a rage."

"The lion?" I said, mystified.

"Myron, my dear, Myron," said Mrs. Ramson, "and I warn you not to get into his path. He's been pacing up and down the drawing room for the last hour."

"Why," I said, sitting down, at Jane's gesture, on one of the radiator seats which seemed warm as though it were reminiscing on the past winter, "I thought this was the night when he held his short-story class in the Garden Room."

"That's just it," said Jane, breaking into a dangerous giggle, while Delia allowed herself a repressed smile, keeping always a lookout from the kitchen door to the closed drawing room beyond the dining room and the hall. ("We carefully planned this vista," Delia would say to a visitor in the drawing room; "see, you can look straight through to my kitchen"; and the listener would look and see a rack of shining red plates and the proud Oxford egg cups all in a row. The shelves of the rack had been carefully measured, Delia would continue to explain, so that they would be "slender enough for beauty but wide enough for use.")

But I was talking about Myron in a rage. "You see," said Mrs. Ramson, explaining, "we had all gone to the Salkers' for dinner."

Often, on the clear green spring evenings, they would drive over to the Salkers', a restaurant at a crossroads on the way to Copely Hill and beyond the next town, which Delia was especially fond of, as the proprietor was a real Englishman of the bluff English inn type and could fry fine chops.

"Oh, and Eric," broke in Jane, "I'm sure I'm going to have a pimple on my nose again" (there was one particular spot which always threatened the pale clarity of her skin), "because I simply had to eat oodles and oodles of whipped cream on my pie."

"Oodles and oodles of whipped cream on my pie."

"Oh, you know you liked it," said Delia with jealous indulgence, for her skin was not so fine-grained as Jane's.

"Well, mother, what do you expect," said Jane, "with that Mr. Salker standing over me twirling his walrus moustaches so I was just too terrified to do anything but eat?"

"But why is Professor Ramson angry?" I asked. "What's the story?"

"I was coming to it," said Delia, "when Jane interrupted me. You know how it is: we haven't been to see the Salkers' since last spring, as I was such an invalid this winter, and I had much to talk over with Mrs. Salker; she wanted to know why Clarence couldn't come, and if the wedding date was set, and so many things."

"Oh, but you know, mother," said Jane, "he simply hasn't a strong stomach and he can't go their heavy food. I feel as if I couldn't eat for a week myself."

"Well," said Mrs. Ramson, ignoring Jane, "we talked and talked, and Myron was smoking his cigar with Mr. Salker, and then, all of a sudden, we looked at the clock, all three of us, and there it was, five minutes to eight. The class was to begin at eight, you know, and Myron didn't say anything but 'Goodbye,' and hustled us out of the restaurant into the car. We flew over the roads, Myron not saying a word, and my heart in my mouth, for never, never, never have we driven so rapidly in our car."

"And then," said Jane, taking up the story, "it was too late anyway, for just as we turned the corner of the road to Otterby we met all the students in a body, and father just turned white and drove on. You know, it's the first class he's missed in ten years."

I recalled then the college tradition that if the professor was later than seven minutes after the hour the students were free to go and the professor was fined five dollars.

"He was just three minutes late," said Delia; "it's really a shame they wouldn't wait, for after all it was my fault."

Myron did not leave the drawing room until it was time to go to bed.

LII

Antony Troy Tarpon, now definitely courting Marian Hoard, had taken up horseback riding as a sport because she liked it, and came to Otterby less frequently. He was resting on his oars a little, for he was sure that he was so solid with Delia that his position was safe.

But his rapid rise into favour and seeming surety of retaining his high place swelled his self esteem, already considerable, to a dangerous volume, and in trying to pull off a magnificent coup, he made one little false step and plunged into obscurity for the rest of the season. It was his last excursion into the arts - that is, music- that was his undoing.

He seemed to have a peculiar gift for selecting the exact moment when he could expect the most attention and sympathy from Delia. So one afternoon he arrived for tea at Otterby dressed in brown more, carefully than usual, and was the sole guest.

"I have pleasant news," he said.

"Oh," said Delia, "you always have; what are you doing now?"

"Nothing in particular, but my dear friend Monsieur Jean-le-Doux and his wife are coming to visit me."

"Who?" asked Delia.

"Why, haven't you heard the name Jean-le Doux?" asked Antony Troy Tarpon in slight surprise.

Delia did not like to be caught ignorant of something she should know, and though she had never heard the name Jean-le-Doux, she made a clever stab.

"Jean-le-Doux," she murmured; "it seems I have heard the name ... but it is so long since I was in France."

"Oh, that explains it," said he, "for as yet he isn't really famous in America. Just in a few of the select musical circles of Boston he is known rather well. I met him in France last year. Of course, in Paris he's recognized as one of the greatest."

"Oh, yes," said Delia vaguely, wondering greatest what.

"He worked for years behind closed doors," said Antony Troy Tarpon impressively, "and when he finally burst on the French musical circles he was immediately recognized as one of the most coherent interpreters of the moderns that the French have ever had."

Delia shuddered instinctively at the word "moderns." "If he belongs to the dissonant, demolishing moderns, I don't want to hear him," said Delia; "that music they write today just unstrings my nerves. Eric was telling me recently - you know he is young, so one must forgive and understand his revolutionary tendencies -- that a young American named ... Anthile, I believe" (Mrs. Ramson owed her social success, she often said, to her exact memory for names), "has written a ballet for nineteen mechanical pianos, three windpipes, and airplane propellers in several sizes, so you can see how sterile these moderns are; no longer able to compose music legitimately, they are turning to pure sensationalism. No, if this friend of yours is a modern ... really, I think I must have been confusing his name with another Frenchman."

George Antheil, composer of Ballet Méchanique. Delia has pronounced his name phonetically as it sounds. His composition does indeed call for airplane propellors. Its first performance caused a riot in Paris.

"Oh, don't be alarmed," said Antony Troy Tarpon; "I was using 'modern' in the true sense of the word, as does Jean-le-Doux-that is, one can admit certain of the early things of Ravel, but from there on music disappears, and we have only a few tricksters fooling about with ill-organized cacaphonies."

"Oh," said Mrs. Ramson, "that's very clever of you, Mr. Tarpon, to ignore the "moderns' completely. Yes, I think I could admit the early Ravel. He wrote the 'Roi d'Ys,' didn't he?"

"The 'Roi d'Ys', repeated Antony Troy Tarpon suavely, "and several other lovely things. Then I must say that Jean-le-Doux converted me to Debussy."

"Debussy ...," mused Mrs. Ramson, not certain whether he should be admitted or not; "he is miasmic, you know ... but he has moments ..." – she paused while Debussy entered the Hall of the Immortals – "moments, you know, when one senses he was a great artist who suffered from, perhaps - how shall I say? - a kind of poppied eroticism ... an inferiority complex tinged with tired Orientalism."

LIII

The upshot of the visit of Antony Troy Tarpon was that, as he had such limited place and means, Mrs. Ramson would have the honour of entertaining Monsieur Jean-le-Doux, the famous pianist, and his wife at dinner just before the concert. For in some manner Antony Troy Tarpon had arranged with the music department to have a concert by Monsieur Jean-le-Doux under its auspices, chiefly because the Frenchman asked no fee and the music department was always in need of money and glad to have free services. The concert was announced in the daily paper as a concert of modern music: from Liszt to Ravel. It was to be in a week's time, and Antony Troy Tarpon lost no time in spreading the news of his friend's approaching visit.

Jean Picart Le Doux (1902-1982) turned to graphic design in 1935 and became a famous artist and tapestry designer. It seems that his earlier life included unsuccessful attempts at music, bookbinding, and publishing, the memory of which has been eclipsed by his later fame.

LIV

Clarence's courtship was a quiet one, of constancy rather than ardour; whenever he was not at work he was with Jane, and they went for long walks together in the night. Once they came back very late and Jane could not get up to her room, for all the doors were closed and could not be opened because all the floors had suddenly been revarnished at the order of Delia, as the first varnish had not been successful. When we had finally moved into Otterby two months after the scheduled time, it was apparent even then that the floors had not been varnished properly, as wherever one stepped, a greyish footprint remained, but Delia could wait no longer to enter, and said the state of the floors "might ameliorate with the passing of time."

It did not, however, and it was I who suffered, for I had to oil-mop the floors daily and at first, during the chic teas, had to go around with a sole of felt on one shoe in order carefully to obliterate the marks made by the distinguished visitors without their knowing it. "Half the comfort of this room", Delia would say to a guest in the drawing room, so as to attract him while I industriously rubbed with my foot, "is due to the sense of 'rest' which comes from the dark-coloured floor and the two steps down. Why do you feel uncomfortable in a New England farmhouse parlour? It's because the floor is light-coloured and flies up in your face, disturbing your equilibrium." Guests would admire the floor then, which at twilight would have liquid depths all around the edges of the yellow Chinese rug sparingly sprinkled with pale blue flowers, and Mrs. Ramson would continue: "We got the recipe for the varnish from an old craftsman of Virginia, from one of those old workers who considered this varnish some holy liquid. I had to coax him a long time before he gave it to me."

But the workmen in Otterby were not such consecrated beings as the old Virginia varnisher, and grumbled at using the old-fashioned recipe. Delia was more obdurate than they, however, and had her way, although the floors were not a practical success until after the second varnishing.

It was sometime in the early morning of that day that Delia abruptly decided to revarnish, and, the idea once in her head, she lost no time in setting it in operation. I did not come home at noon that day, so I did not know about her decision, and when I did arrive late in the afternoon, following a baseball game which we had lost badly - Mrs. Ramson had said the day before that she would be too ill the next day to serve tea, so that I could be excused - no one was at home, for both Myron and Delia had gone to the game also (as I learned later), and I entered by the kitchen way. I had made three steps into the dining room before I discovered that the floor was sticky and that I had left an Indian trail behind me. Standing on one foot, like a surprised stork, I realized at length what must have happened in Delia's mind, for she had been living so quietly the two weeks previous. It was always that way with her, rhythmic periods of serenity followed by violent changes and reforms. But I knew it would do no good to stand at the threshold of the dining room in the waning light of the orchid curtains, and, deciding that retreat was the lesser evil, I carefully retraced my steps, which had turned silvery on the linoleum floor of the kitchen. Just as I stepped out of the kitchen door, Delia and Myron drove down the driveway and Delia saw me standing there guiltily.

"Eric, you didn't enter the house?" she asked, imploring and menacing at the same moment.

"I'm sorry, but I did," I answered. "I didn't know that you had had the floors varnished again."

"If you had reported at noon," said Delia, nettled - noon-reporting was a duty she had invented at the moment - "this would not have happened. Never in all my life have I been able to keep people from walking on my floors when they are wet with varnish. If it isn't the butcher boy, it's the butler. I suppose you walked all the way through the house."

"No," I said, "just through the kitchen, and a few steps in the dining room."

Myron, who had come up during the last part of Delia's talk, said then, "Oh, that's not so bad, my dear; it could be worse, you know; you mustn't fume - it's not good for your heart and besides, if a thing is done, it's done."

"That's all very well," said Delia, "but you don't have to face those terrifying workmen. They get as angry as can be, and then they refuse to listen to my instructions even when I stand over them, for they lose their confidence in me when they see there is no coöperation with the members of the family."

"Never mind, I will speak to the workmen myself to-morrow morning," said Myron.

Delia calmed down under his soothing voice and promise, saying, "The irony of it! We came back expressly to warn you, Eric, and our car was not as fast as your feet."

"My dear," said Myron, "you are losing your sense of relationships; if you had not stopped to talk to Mrs. Heron ..."

"If you had only pinned a note to the door," I added.

"Oh, I dislike that sort of thing," said Mrs. Ramson. "I was using a bit of subtle psychology instead, but it just shows that psychology doesn't work. You see, I had the workmen put the ladder up to your window sill." I looked and saw the ladder for the first time- "and I reasoned: Eric is a boy; he won't be able to look at a ladder up to his room without climbing it. "

Myron laughed gently. "My dear, my dear, what a capital story for Marsh!"

They drove off then to dine and took me along with them as far as Main Street, where I got off to go to the hash house made famous by Edna St. Vincent Millay.

Late that night, when I was safely ensconced in bed, having entered in the unusual way - as Delia and Myron must have entered also an hour before (I did not see them, but heard them talking in their room together) - and was reading by a lamp at my side, Jane and Clarence came down the drive.

"Eric," called Jane softly and clearly, "are you awake?"

"Yes," I answered. "Have Mr. Rollinson hold the ladder, because it's rickety."

I did not listen to what they said to each other; besides, they talked in very low tones, and it took them a long, long time to say goodbye.

Then I heard Jane come up the ladder rungs nimbly. The window casing made a picture frame for her as she extended her smartly slippered foot over the sill and then came smiling in with a little jump from the dark.

"Thank you so much for waiting," she said to me as she left the room. "Clarence was so worried that I wouldn't be able to get in: mother does make the maddest arrangements, you know."

"It was a pleasure to wait," I said. "Good night."

"Good night,' she answered very, very sweetly.

My door clicked shut, and a little later all Otterby was still.

LV

I opened the door for Monsieur Jean-leDoux and his wife, saying, "Bon soir," as Antony Troy Tarpon, who followed just behind them, had warned us they spoke scarcely a word of English; "Monsieur le Professeur Ramson va descendre tout de suite"; and then, after I had assisted Madame Jean-le-Doux with her wraps, I opened the drawing-room door to the room which was cool and shadowed, decorated with tall lilies, waxy-coloured in the light of the candles- saying, "Voulez-vous entrer par ici, s'il vous plaît?" Antony Troy Tarpon sent a questioning glance after me as he entered, for he did not know I spoke French, and I returned his look with a bland, cold smile.

I went into the drawing room a few moments after telling Myron and Delia the guests had arrived, to close the curtains I had purposely left open (they closed by pulling a silken cord, like a stage curtain) so that I might get a good look at the guests.

Even in the soft candlelight, Madame Jean-le-Doux's face was floridly red, and whatever way she turned or sat, she was all plump curves. Her eyes were bright and brown as she talked about the awful train they had come up on. The train was a famous one, as it stopped at every cow path and in betweeen made mad progress rolling like a boat. She was chatting in a Parisian French all the time, rapidly and with many elisions, going almost completely over the head of Antony Troy Tarpon, who murmured, at inappropriate intervals, "Tiens, tiens," or "C'est vrai?"

Monsieur Jean-le-Doux sat in the quiet glow of the red ribbon in his buttonhole, a small man of fine features and tranquil hands. He refused a cigarette from Antony Troy Tarpon and did not join in the conversation or even seem to listen. He was like a cat, which, entering a strange room, is not comfortable until it has absorbed the strangeness by looking carefully all over and noting all the room's details.

Myron came down then and his graciousness charmed the French people; he could not understand them very well, as he spoke their language with little facility, and essayed to speak in Portuguese, which he spoke perfectly, and Monsieur Jean-le-Doux visibly brightened on hearing that tongue, as he also spoke it, though he halted for words as Myron had done in French. During the war Myron did a great deal of translating Portuguese documents for the government, and Mrs. Ramson was very proud of this, as "despite his age Myron showed himself to be a true soldier, for he loved his country like a gentleman."

The dinner was a strange one, for the guests, excepting Monsieur Jean-le-Doux, seemed to have so much to say to each other, and Mrs. Ramson had Antony Troy Tarpon floundering vainly several times in an effort to tell Madame Jean-le-Doux how highly Mrs. Ramson considered the French cuisine, but didn't she think that the addition of a few Italian plates was an improvement?

Madame Jean-le-Doux, finally comprehending, showed herself to be a real Frenchwoman by saying brightly that Italian dishes were good for Italians and that the French cuisine was incapable of improvement. With such a flat denial ("Denying is part of the French temperament," Delia said one day long after), she turned her attention to Monsieur, who, however, was becoming more and more palpably nervous as the clock-hands were turning to the hour of his concert, and begged with his eyes for silence. The train had been so late he had not had time to practice a few moments even on the piano he was to play on that evening, and he was filled with apprehension.

His emotion must have flowered violently when he first put his hands to the keys; never have I heard a grand piano so unpleasantly out of tune. The music department had printed programs, but there their attention had ended. From the distaste on his face as he touched the keys, I surmised that they were dirty as well as jangling. The first number he played was a long sonata by Liszt, and to the horror of the audience and himself, many of the strings did not sound at all and many sounded with an irritating buzz.

Despite all the publicity Antony Troy Tarpon had given the concert, the huge assembly hall was pitifully bare, and Monsieur Jean-le-Doux having requested that there be as low lighting as possible, the hall was filled with shadows and seemed anything but gay.

Before the concert began, Antony Troy Tarpon appeared on the platform and gave a long introductory talk on the "true moderns," demolishing Stravinsky and his cohorts in a single phrase, "We do not recognize the 'modern' murderers of music," and I caught sight that moment of Mrs. Rosenkrantz, who was listening enraptured. Had there been more light, I think she would have dared a bravo.

Igor Stravinsky was called "a modern murderer of music".

Monsieur Jean-le-Doux vainly tried to seduce his instrument to something like music all through the Liszt, but it was not until he had reached Ravel that he had learned how to hide the numerous faults of the piano, and though he played "Les Oiseaux Tristes" a trifle sentimentally, it was obvious that he was a competent pianist and not insensitive.

Mrs. Ramson was in raptures over him at a reception held next door in Mrs. Rosenkrantz's house immediately after the concert. "What technique!

What soul!" she repeated over and over again, while munching one of Mrs. Rosenkrantz's "original" dainties, the now famous candied carrots.

He played a great deal more at Mrs. Rosenkrantz's in the pleasure of finding a real instrument under his hands, and once, in between numbers, he said to Mrs. Ramson, who hovered over him constantly like an immense benevolent butterfly, "Mon père m'a toujours dit, quand j'ai mal joué, que ce n'était pas le piano mais le pianiste; quand même," he laughed with gentle irony, "Ce soir je crois que ce n'était pas le pianiste qui avait tort."

LVI

The blow fell a week later. Antony Troy had almost forgotten the Jean-le Douxs and the concert in a violent but unsuccessful attempt to revive the ancient sport of archery. He never dreamed he had mismanaged the visit of his French friends, and was basking in the sun of Delia's approval with smug contentment.

In the morning mail, which was always voluminous, as Myron received letters from all parts of the world; and though he was a desultory letter writer, cleaning up his correspondence about once every two months with one fell sweep in an afternoon and night, he continued to receive a great deal of mail, was a simple little envelope from the town garage, containing a narrow yellow slip which read:

Taxi (night May 10th) $20.00
(Referred to you by Mr. A. T. Tarpon)

Mrs. Ramson called up the garage to verify the bill (which had come with a flock of others), in a strange state of excitement, and, finding it to be exact, wrote an extra sweet note to Antony Troy Tarpon to come that day to tea.

It was a tea like the one she had had for Clarence, many flowers and sandwiches, and Jasmine Flower in the silver pot and alone. I never knew exactly what passed behind the doors of the drawing room then, but I know Antony Troy Tarpon was still explaining volubly as he left, but the suave tone of his voice was a little harsh with nervousness and his phrases a little ragged with fear. He never had the opportunity of paying for the ill-fated taxi, while Mrs. Ramson paid it grimly, saying it was worth the price to know the nature of the man.

Antony Troy Tarpon did not show up again at Otterby, and at the end of the year (as he had entrenched himself so solidly in the town) he was transferred to another department of the college.

LVII

Mrs. Ramson always went to Boston in the spring to order her high-buttoned shoes, and always returned very tired but ravished with what she had seen.

She always visited the museum there. "The curator of the Oriental department was so kind to me, Myron, and he showed me a wonderful tapestry eighteen feet long and a foot wide, Chinese, with waves and waves" - Delia described great wavelike gestures - "and the most terrifying dragons in the world. It was like standing before one of the Old Masters for the first time… you remember, dear, when we saw "The Last Supper" on our honeymoon together? … And there was a beautiful Italian statue too, a figure recumbent in sleep. Sleeping but just on the point of waking up. Oh, it was delicious!"

All this conversation was at dinner, which was furthermore distinguished by the presence of young Douglas MacNeil. Antony Troy Tarpon was a shattered idol and Mrs. Ramson had swept him out of mind. Feeling an absence, however, she was not long in filling it, and the lightning struck on young MacNeil, who had been keeping so quiet all year that no one had noticed him except Myron, and Myron was pleased.

He was a Montana boy, a graduate of the college; it was rather exceptional that he be admitted so quickly to the teaching staff, but he was an exceptional person. Small of stature but well-knit and strong, he had a way of effacing himself in a drawing room till, as Mrs. Ramson exclaimed, "like the Cheshire Cat, you could only see his smile!" His smile was a very sensitive and crooked one, for his lips were finely moulded and seldom still.

He wrote poetry that Myron said "had the streak of genius," rather imagistic verse but very vivid; I remember Myron read one in the drawing room one night after dinner to Delia, about a cloud careening in the ocean like a sinking ship, while a star slowly wound a spool of thin red fire.

"He lacks the reliability that would make a good professor," said Myron, "and I do not think the college is the best place for a poet to develop in. But he has shown me chapters of a novel he is writing now, and it seems to me the best poetic prose I have ever read."

Delia, pricking up her ears at this, invited MacNeil especially to come one evening and read some of his work for her. She began to feel very romantic about having a novel born under the roofs of Otterby, and when the young man finally arrived, very timid, for he knew there was no escape and detested Scarot as much as he feared him, Mrs. Ramson was in a state to be overwhelmed, and before the first chapter was finished, she was.

"Oh, Eric!" she exclaimed over the sandwiches the next day; "you must try to know this MacNeil boy, for he is so lonely and has a streak of genius."

"I heard Professor Ramson say he was writing an interesting novel," I replied. "He seems like a very nice fellow."

"Oh, his novel is superb," said Mrs. Ramson, "the best of the year! It is more than a novel; it is a drama in Montana of great spiritual forces."

The novel had a sad history. MacNeil was not without temperament, and, finding the atmosphere of the town oppressively heavy with thinking heads, increasing in density as the examination date neared, he took a flying trip to New York to write his last chapter there.

The night before he returned someone forgot to stamp out a cigarette in the corridor of his shambly boarding house, and house and novel shot up in flames. The fire was a fine one, sparks flying up a mile high, and the students stood about cheering as the firemen worked like mad.

His brother told him the next day at the station what had happened.

"What's the matter, kid? You look so glum," said MacNeil.

"Your novel's burnt up," his brother said.

MacNeil said nothing about the loss to any one, but the same day he learned of it he played a game of handball with Professor Marsh, who was champion of the courts, and trounced him so soundly that everyone was amazed.

"You had better not burn up any more novels," said Professor Marsh to him (the story had appeared in the morning paper), highly amused at this psychological example of sublimation.

After that episode he settled down to rewriting the novel, and Mrs. Ramson said the Garden Room was open to him any week night except Tuesday to work in. He came quite often and Mrs. Ramson always made him coffee, she was so pleased to have someone writing in Otterby, "for the more living and creating that goes on inside its walls, the richer and more beautiful a house it will be." He stayed several times to sleep even, Mrs. Ramson making sure he was "comfy" in the beautiful guest room.

This room was not large but it was the most glowing, comfortable room I have ever seen. The walls were of a special rough texture of plaster, a foundation of dull rose faintly veiled over with a coat of peach, while the floor was a warm dull red. The blue Chinese rug glowed softly by comparison. The furniture was cream coloured, and there was a little niche in the wall above the bed for a crucifix, as the room was a Spanish one.

There were no pictures, for the Ramsons did not take kindly to them; they preferred beautiful walls. The only ornament was a photograph of Jane that she had had taken in Washington, with her lips pursed in a provocative pout. These bright spring days she seemed to be more beautiful every morning. Her wedding was to be towards the end of June in the sunken garden, and one afternoon she called me into her room to show me the wedding dress she had providentially bought in Paris ahead of her engagement. It was from Lanvin's, a kind of shepherdess dress in pale blue with wide bouffant skirts of lace coloured écru.

Otterby was quietly humming with all the activity which precedes a wedding: all kinds of long conferences with Delia in regard to invitations, guests, and menus, long talks and walks with Clarence, and sewing from morning to night. Besides, Mr. and Mrs. Spinner, Delia's parents, were coming up a few days ahead of the wedding, and Mrs. Ramson, who dreaded this first visit of inspection, began to see dust where no dust was, she got such a mania for cleaning, and life in Otterby became difficult.

Indeed, she became very tired, and one warm night, while sitting outside on the Garden Room terrace alone after coffee-Myron had gone up to his study for a while-she was half asleep and a strange thing happened.

She was sitting in the great wicker armchair with arm rests that sloped deeply to the stone. Hearing the faint patter of animal feet on the terrace, she reached out her hand, saying, "Here, Scarot," and stroked a furry back. Oh, it was not Scarot, for Scarot was not furry; it must be little Rags, Professor Curman's dog, come from next door to be sociable.

"Nice Rags, nice Rags," Delia murmured, stroking with gentle constancy; "nice Rags... nice... " but was it Rags?

A horrible premonition seized her heart. The air was suddenly saturated with a strange, strong odor, and, looking down at her hand, Delia choked a scream that might have split the eaves of Otterby. For all the while she had been caressing, not little Rags, but a skunk!

Cold with horror, she leaned back, trembling in the chair, while the skunk, scenting Scarot, who was off nosing for mice in the attic, walked with measured pace off the terrace to the thin birch wood that fringed the pond.

Delia reached down and stroked the skunk without seeing it, thinking it was her little dog.

LVIII

Mrs. Ramson had scarcely recovered from this incident when another shock of greater import occurred. Robert Frost was coming to town again! Myron would not hear of the doors of Otterby being closed on the man whom he considered the finest poet in America, and so, there being no alternative, Mrs. Ramson rose to the occasion superbly.

Robert Frost was coming to see them again, "the finest poet in America."

He came a little after noon, a most unpropitious hour, for Delia dearly loved her after luncheon nap. Myron, too, who had been living on toast for the last month - he was always in bad shape at the end of the school year, for there was too much work then - by doctor's orders had to take a nap before and after luncheon. "A simple siesta," Delia would remark, "is one of Nature's greatest restoratives. It enables you to retain your morning freshness straight through tea until dinner." But, of course, Frost's early arrival put the quietus on the siesta for that day. Sleep would have been a waste of precious moments better spent by far in the invigorating presence of a poet who, for Delia, had become overnight "the finest in the world."

The dinner seemed dull, as no one dressed, and Myron, in a dark blue suit, was rather uncomfortable, not only because he had to pretend he was eating with the rest, but because he did not have that assurance in his conversation which a stiff shirt always gave him. By degrees, however, the dinner heightened in interest as the guests loosened their minds down to the point of the poet's mental relaxation. "Something there is that doesn't love a wall."

Jessie came for coffee because Mrs. Ramson knew she knew Frost, so she had a secure excuse to Mrs. Heron for the invitation. Jessie had met the poet at her father's house in Canada, and the two were sympathetic spirits.

She played Händel that night, the Sonata in D Major, and Frost was highly pleased. "How direct music is!" he said. "Not a word or a page between you and the listener; the emotion goes right over without a halt."

Oh, but I meant to say-in serving coffee I established a new tradition for Otterby quite by accident. Preparing for the arrival of her mother, Mrs. Spinner, Mrs. Ramson the day before had routed all the silver of the house out on the dining-room table, and we spent half the afternoon cleaning it. Almost all the silver was solid, but there was one tiny spoon made of tin. I examined it. It was a souvenir spoon of the Chicago World Exposition with a blue bar around the handle. I showed it to Mrs. Ramson. She was surprised. "Why, how did that get there!" she exclaimed. "It must have come from Bishop Ramson. Put it to one side, Eric; I'll show it to Myron later."

But in the confusion of preparing sandwiches and tea right afterwards, I forgot about it and put it in with the other coffee spoons.

And it was that spoon that turned up on Robert Frost's saucer, and I saw it just too late, just as I handed the coffee to him. I told Mrs. Ramson of my mistake immediately, and she rectified it as quickly by a bold move.

"Mr. Frost," she said, breaking into the middle of a conversation he was having with Jessie - and anyway she did not want Jessie to be "monopolizing" this "greatest lion of the year" even for five minutes, because she said young people were so "tiring to a great man's mind; they take with both hands and give nothing back but impertinence" - "Mr. Frost," she interrupted again, this time securing his attention, "you see the spoon you have?"

"Yes," said Frost, looking at the spoon for the first time, as he had not stirred his coffee. "Yes," he said, turning it over in his hand, somewhat mystified.

"That's the special celebrity spoon of Otterby!"

Myron looked up from his conversation with Mrs. Adams, who was also one of the coffee guests, with surprise and slight terror, for he was always afraid Delia would put her foot in it, the evening had been going altogether too well.

"You see," said Delia, started in earnest, "it's made of tin, while all the other guests' spoons are made of silver. Its value is a spiritual one; we cherish it because dear Bishop Ramson gave it to us with his own hands." Her tone became impressive; Delia had become the lady of the landed estate. "And when a person comes to visit us whom we cherish and who we realize has some of that same spiritual force which distinguished Bishop Ramson while he was among us, we serve his coffee with this little spoon."

The moment was a religious one, and no one knew what to say. Myron was astounded, Frost a trifle embarrassed, Jessie speechless. Mrs. Adams tried to say, "How charming!" but she only mumbled something. The tension of the room was fortunately relieved at that moment by the doorbell sounding.

It was Professor and Mrs. Busby and their little girl of five, Suzanne. Professor Busby, of the English department, a quiet, dull scholar, had been chosen by Clarence to be best man at the wedding, and Delia, who had heretofore received the Busbys on official occasions only, took the opportunity of Frost's visit to serve as a peg for the quiet formal call.

Mrs. Busby, a pretty, frail woman with brown eyes, had no idea why Suzanne was to be brought along, but Mrs. Ramson was so insistent that the little girl come that Mrs. Busby agreed, reasoning that where Mrs. Ramson was concerned, obedience was the best policy.

"Oh, I'm so glad you've come!" said Mrs. Ramson, greeting them on their entrance. The Busbys knew everyone in the room except Mr. Frost, and Mrs. Ramson lost no time in introducing them, this time quite cutting Jessie out of the picture. "Mr. Frost, I want you to meet Professor Busby and his wife. Professor Busby is one of Myron's men who hides his light under a bushel but who's really very brilliant. He's soon to become almost a member of our family, for he's to be best man at the wedding I told you about this afternoon." (Clarence and Jane were absent for the evening, as Clarence was ill and Jane had gone over to his room with Mrs. Fife to read to him.)

Frost shook hands with the guests, smiling gravely.

"And now," said Delia triumphantly, "here is little Suzanne, whom we had almost forgotten." The little girl, dressed in a bright little frock of yellow to match her hair, her brown eyes opened wide to be sure she was awake at this forbidden hour, looked up into the poet's face with a quick, timid smile. He was touched with this gesture of friendliness and, sitting down, took the child on his lap, asking what was her name. "Thuthanne Peabody Buthby."

All the guests laughed politely, while Mrs. Ramson whispered audibly to Mrs. Busby, "I knew, my dear, that he would take her on his lap; that's why I wanted you to bring her so. All great, simple men love children, and now, when she grows up, you can tell her that when she was little she sat on the lap of a great poet!"

Jessie played again then, bits of the ballet "Scheherazade," which she knew Myron loved. "Rimsky-Korsakoff has such quality, such Oriental grace," he would say lusciously, as though he were tasting the music.

Delia talked a long while with Mrs. Adams, who at that moment was a centre of sympathy in the town. Her son Jack had broken all the traditions of the town families by announcing that a professor's life was a dog's life, that college was stupid, and that he would not enter it, and clinched his statement by quitting the home and going to Boston to work in a garage.

"This afternoon," said Mrs. Ramson, "when I took Mr. Frost upstairs to show him his room, he stopped for a full minute before the three ships in the wall and quoted the first verse of Masefield's poem about them.' The three ships formed a bas-relief in plaster, on the wall, of three Spanish galleons, and they made a beautiful decoration. All over the house, in various odd corners, were these ships sailing in pure colour, and in the Garden Room there was a thistle and a rose, the emblem of the Ramson family.

Robert Frost stopped for a full minute, looked at the three ships, and quoted John Masefield.

Finally, everyone having finished with coffee and cigarettes, there was the lull Myron had been impatiently waiting for, and he launched his special request and the request of all his guests that Mr. Frost read from his own works. On the table at his side were, neatly piled, the slender volumes.

Frost accepted simply and without hesitation. He did not use the books but recited from memory. "I think," he said, "I will begin with my last poem, 'New Hampshire.' It is a kind of outburst. I wrote it when I was fed up with Greenwich Village."

There was a holy silence while he recited in a grey, monotonous voice, the soft candlelight lighting his grey hair that curled in a careless fall over his forehead, shadowing his half closed eyes. When he came to the words "sons of bitches", Mrs. Ramson quivered violently. But no one saw her apologetic smile and she fell to listening once again, more enwrapt than before, her nervous fingers slowly rolling a cigarette to ruin.

LIX

Delia had made a most terrifying myth of her mother to me: I even dreamt about a little lady with glasses crying in malicious glee at finding a microscopic spot on the windowpane. But, for all the inspection that took place, our efforts were in vain. Mr. and Mrs. Spinner were very simple people who arrived very tired from travelling and immediately presented a Smithfield Ham that had been smoked in their own smokehouse.

"Oh, Eric," said Mrs. Ramson magnanimously, "you'll have a taste of ham you have never tasted before! Mama is one of the few persons in Virginia who still retain the priceless secret of authentic smoking."

An authentic Smithfield Ham, according to the old Virginia recipe.

Mrs. Spinner was a vigorous, generously built woman with a direct way of talking. She found the electric stove "newfangled", and expressed strong doubts as to its cooking properties. It was clear she did not understand her daughter, and Delia's phrases and voluminous explanations left her in a fog. "You seem to be well situated", she said finally "and you seem happy, so I'm satisfied."

Mr. Spinner, bald-headed and spare, said little. He startled poor little Mrs. Soccy nearly out of her wits at luncheon (she was one of the few guests) by saying that her sketches of Otterby had multum in parvo. As she did not know the phrase was Latin, she thought it was something unpleasant and turned a despairing countenance to Mrs. Ramson, who came to the rescue by addressing her father playfully, "You charming old scholars with your Latin phrases! Much in little, indeed! We all think Mrs. Soccy's sketches are charming moments caught by her fleeting pencil for all time."

Mr. Spinner did not reply, but a little later he said to his wife, "This ham is not so good as I've tasted at home. Are you sure you took the right one?"

"Of course," assured Mrs. Spinner with asperity. "It's not the ham; it's Delia's newfangled electric stove."

"Mama, how you talk!" said Delia. "The stove has nothing to do with it. I just haven't got the precision of your hand."

"Delicious!" exploded Myron (who had broken his diet to taste it). "I couldn't imagine more delicious ham."

"Now, papa," said Delia, "you must be still, for it's a connoisseur of food says the ham is delicious, and that ends the matter."

"All right, my daughter," said Mr. Spinner, "I'll lay it to the climate."

And they all laughed.

LX

Jane and Clarence came into the family tea at four-thirty; Mrs. Ramson had expressly kept them away until that time, for she said it would be too overwhelming for Mr. and Mrs. Spinner to meet the whole family all at once.

The wedding was only a few days off now, and Jane went about the house singing snatches of songs, and though she was bright to see, she was seldom attentive to what was being said.

Mrs. Spinner was satisfied with Jane's appearance, and she had known Clarence for a long time. She was satisfied with Clarence, too, though she did not think the match a particularly brilliant one. Clarence was even more discreet than usual, as though he was afraid something might happen to spoil the wedding. He took a cigar (he detested smoking them) from Mr. Spinner, and lit it with pleasure so carefully simulated that only Delia saw through it.

"I thought you detested cigars," she said sweetly to him.

"Detest cigars!" exclaimed Mr. Spinner, looking at Clarence intently.

"Oh, no! Oh, no!" said Clarence easily, while it was with difficulty that he kept from blushing. "I don't smoke them often, but now and again" - puffing a little obviously - "it's a real pleasure."

Delia just looked at him.

Scarot changed the subject then by leaping in the air and barking by the window sill.

"Oh, precious, precious, he wants his collar!" exclaimed Jane at the questioning glances of Mr. and Mrs. Spinner. "Did we forget to dress him up for grandma and grandpa! Did we forget!" And she fastened the collar around his black neck. It was a collar she had bought in Paris, of orange leather studded with silver knobs and ruffed with a white flare of stiff hair. Scarot looked like a caricature of an Elizabethan courtier in it, and was extremely proud of himself. They all laughed at him, he strutted so.

"You know what Booth Tarkington says about dogs," said Delia. "It's true; they keep a family in good humour."

Booth Tarkington said that dogs keep a family in good humour.

"But where did he get the collar?" asked Mrs. Spinner. "I never saw the like."

"Oh, in Paris, where all nice things come from," said Jane lightly.

"Newfangled notions," grunted Mr. Spinner. "Paris!"

Then the Busbys and some other people dropped in, and the talk shifted to Virginia and how the Rotary Club was ruining the state by advertising through the mail so that all sorts of strange people, Yankees and what not, were drifting in.

LXI

It was the day before the wedding, a moment in the afternoon, one of those strange moments snatched out of time's reach, being so disconnected with the events of the day. I was standing in the drawing room with Mrs. Ramson, and had just finished mopping for the third time that day, while she had just finished arranging the roses. Everywhere you looked there were roses. Jane and Clarence were away for a walk before tea, Mr. and Mrs. Spinner and Myron were taking an afternoon nap, and Otterby was utterly quiet. I just stood looking at the lovely room, resting on my mop haphazardly, while Mrs. Ramson stood by the window where the vase of blue Venetian glass she had brought back so carefully from her honeymoon glowed like something alive. She looked over the landscape and sighed. "How tired I am!" she said. "How glad I will be when this wedding is over!"

"Ah, yes," I said, looking out to the green hills, too.

"Oh, when they are finally gone and we can take a deep breath," she exclaimed, "Myron and I will go out to the hills and lie on the grass all day! I hope you too, Eric," she said, suddenly becoming tender, "I hope you can go out to the hills this summer. You need it."

Something displeased her in the roses of the Venetian vase and she fumbled a moment with the flowers, pulling up a bit of fern. "Yes, you must get out to the hills, Eric," she repeated. "Everyone needs it."

And then, solemnly, looking me straight in the eyes, she said, "Nature is food for the soul."

GARNES, FRANCE, July 4, 1927.

The Ivy League Dartmouth College, at Hanover, New Hampshire, where these events happened. Below, the annual Commencement Exercise, which happens at the end of each academic year.